WANDOR THE CRUSADER

"Go and seek these: the Helm of Jagnar, the Axe of Yeroda, the Spear of Valkath, the Sword of Artos, the Dragon-Steed of Morkol. Go among all peoples and through all lands and against all who torment and distress men, wherever you find them barring your passage."

Thus speaks the mystic voice of the vast wall of flame, deep underground, sending Wandor the swordsman out to prove that he is the rightful heir to the High Throne of the Hills. It is the beginning of an epic journey across a war-torn medieval landscape—a lone crusade to bring peace and justice against the forces of evil, witchcraft and corruption.

Other Avon Books by
Roland Green

WANDOR'S JOURNEY   24372 $.95

WANDOR'S RIDE

ROLAND GREEN

Roland J. Green

◆ AVON
PUBLISHERS OF BARD, CAMELOT, DISCUS, EQUINOX AND FLARE BOOKS.

WANDOR'S RIDE is an original publication of Avon Books.
This work has never before appeared in any form.

AVON BOOKS
A division of
The Hearst Corporation
959 Eighth Avenue
New York, New York 10019

Copyright © 1973 by Avon Books.
Published by arrangement with the author.

ISBN: 0-380-00575-1

First Avon Printing, July, 1973.
Third Printing

AVON TRADEMARK REG. U.S. PAT. OFF. AND
FOREIGN COUNTRIES, REGISTERED TRADEMARK—
MARCA REGISTRADA, HECHO EN CHICAGO, U.S.A.

Printed in the U.S.A.

I

Bertan Wandor's horse was nearing the top of the long climb up the forested hillside when it suddenly staggered and went down in a flurry of dust and gravel, to lie in the road twitching feebly. He cursed aloud in three languages, then rose, brushing the dust from his leather breeches and tunic. He drew his sword and looked west down the road.

It stretched away into the lengthening shadows, speckled here and there with patches of reddening light that found a way through the forest canopy. It was silent and empty. For a moment, Wandor's hopes rose. Had his pursuers abandoned the chase, having even more reason than he to fear spending the night here in the Hill Forests? He knelt, with one ear to the road, then rose—and cursed again. The roll and boom of many sets of hooves came clearly through the earth, swelling even as he listened.

His horse, he saw at a glance, was dead. To drag it from the road into the bushes was impossible; instead, he pulled his dagger from its sheath and quickly slashed through the straps of his saddlebags. Lifting them in his arms, he slipped across the road into the shadow of the trees and began to select from them what he would need, flicking the unwanted items into the pine needles on the ground.

Sword in its tooled scabbard, dagger in its sheath on his broad copper-studded belt with the weighted buckle, throwing knives in their sheathes on his knee-high riding boots with their flared tops and silver spurs. Not the best thing for forest travel, those boots. He stopped for a moment to pull them off, slipping the throwing knives into his belt. His long-toed bare feet, soles hardened by summer runs through the rolling hills around Trorim, and by long hours of barefoot practice at the House of the Duelists, would take him farther and faster through the woods and leave fewer trails to lead pursuers after him.

Now—blanket roll on his back, strapped low to free arms and shoulders for fighting, and, in the roll, hard biscuit, salt, dried meat, firekit, needles and thread—everything to keep a man alive in the woods. Waterbottle hooked on to his belt, sharkskin climbing buskins around his bare calves. The great five-foot bow and its quiver of arrows—to slay beasts for food and men for safety, if needed. And, finally, a small silk packet, bound in gold thread.

He opened it, and the last rays of the sun blazed on the silver mounting and emerald stones and ruddy gold chain. The emblem of a House Master of the Order of Duelists. A great thing to wear at any time, a wonderous thing to wear at twenty-eight, an ordained thing for any Master of the Order to wear whenever he might have to fight to kill. The emblem thumped his chest as he slipped the chain around his neck. Now came the cloak with its massive wrought-iron clasp, flowing from his broad shoulders down a tree-straight back. And then he was slipping away, south into the forest, away from the road, away from those who pursued him. It was written in the Book of the Five Gods that only the unrighteous fear to face those who come upon them, or seek them out—but the Book of the Five was written in the Ancient Days, when honor and simplicity were the laws men lived under. Now, many of the most righteous in the whole Kingdom of Benzos had fled before the men of Duke Cragor.

Who else, Wandor asked himself as he raced along, but Duke Cragor could conjure a swarm of mounted men from the huts of Trorim to send in headlong pursuit along the Benzor High Road after a solitary Master Duelist? And granted that a swarm was a wise thing, if one were going to carry the pursuit through the forests where the Sthi—the Hill People—clung to their caves and their ancient way of death to all intruders—why pursue such a one at all? Wandor was a House Master, to be sure, but Master of a House that counted scarcely fifteen full Duelists, half again as many apprentices, and only that handful of servants needed to spare the Duelists the most degrading forms of manual labor. And the message he had received from the

Grand Master in Benzor—"Come at once on the business of the Order"—how was that different from messages to House Masters and ordinary Duelists through all the hundreds of years since the dim distant days of the founding of the Order? And if there was any difference, why had he not been told—and how had Cragor discovered it?

Wandor stopped suddenly as a black, cold thought struck him. Cragor was whispered, with perhaps much truth, to have Black Sorcerers at his command. Through their arts, there was little or nothing he could not know if he wished. Yet why then had he not simply called upon them to have Wandor slain or his mind charmed away, if the Duelist held some danger to him?

Wandor knew he would find no answer to these questions here, in the endless miles of forest and hill, and no answers anywhere ever, if his pursuers ever caught up with him. He looked back down the way he had come. Only a few tumbled patches in the needles showed his passage, yet Cragor's men might well be expert enough in woodcraft to track him with even these few clues.

Behind him the sound of hooves rose to a massed thunder, then stopped abruptly. Angry voices came floating up to him. Then the hooves began again, fewer now. The men had divided, some no doubt to plunge directly into the forest, some to move up the road and spread out along a wide front. This was no casual or unskilled pursuit.

It would take them a few minutes to get their search under way, time for him to climb a good stout tree and find out exactly where he was and the best way he might take to escape. There was such a tree just ahead—an immense red shagbark, five men thick with its top lost in the gathering shadows of the forest roof. He strode over to it and began to climb.

The buskins, and his own superbly trained muscles, took him up the tree in five minutes. He had judged well— the stout branch he straddled jutted out into space above the topmost leaves of the nearby trees. His view was clear —but the sight was not pleasing.

Less than two hundred yards away, the road looped through the forest and over the crest of the hill, and all along it, for half a mile in either direction, horses stood tethered to bushes, their riders standing with drawn weapons beside them. The riders were all true Hond stock— tall and blond and straight, like all of Cragor's men—but even at this distance Wandor's eyes noticed in them the hunched brutality of hired bravos and the well-used harnesses and weapons of experienced fighters.

Wandor shifted on his perch to look in the opposite direction—and his stomach went cold and heavy. A mile away, the forest was cut off knife-sudden by a rock wall soaring sheer for three hundred feet. And beyond, a tumbled wilderness of crags and boulders and ravines rising steadily to twin peaks glowing red in the sunset, with a mighty cleft between them plunging away into blue-black night.

This time, Wandor did not curse. He clung to the branch until the pounding of his heart and the coldness in his stomach were gone, and prayed to all the Five Gods for guidance and mercy. The twin peaks he knew to be Mount Pendwyr, and the cleft between them, it was said, led down to the Black Caves of the Hill People. Here was the heart of their most ancient rites, and *here* strangers were given not merely death, but, according to all the legends, a death of horror so far beyond the imagination of civilized men that there were no words for it. And yet it was toward that brooding mountain that Wandor knew he would have to go.

Unless. . . . He sprang from the branch to the ridged trunk, and as he scrambled downward, he saw his one chance was to reach the ground as fast as he could, then break across country toward either end of the line that would soon be moving into the forest to trap him against the cliffs.

As he dropped toward the lower branches, he cast a final look at the road. Yes—there they went, stepping away from their horses, crossing the road, vanishing behind a screen of greenery. He had only minutes to spare. He began to swing downward even faster, yet it still seemed hours before his feet finally thudded again on the solid ground.

Now he was off again, heading east, heading for the farther end of the line being drawn around him. Branches clawed along his cheeks, leaving drops of blood oozing from the tanned skin; roots wrenched at his ankles, sending him reeling forward; snakes and small creeping things scattered from before his racing feet; birds screamed upward in flashes of wings. That would mark his passage, but even if he came upon the enemy, so long as they were only two or three together. . . . His hand dropped to his sword hilt.

8

The ground was sloping down again, he realized. The slope became sharper, and still sharper—and suddenly his feet went out from under him and he was rolling, crashing down through bushes, jarring arms and legs on tree trunks as he hurtled down a near vertical slope. For a moment, blackness swirled around him, as his head struck a stone, then with a crash and a thud he burst out of the bushes to sprawl full-length on sand.

He raised his swimming head to look—to look at what might be the place of his death. From the foot of the cliff, visible through the gap in the trees, a ravine slashed downward through the forest and deep into the rock. Around the gray boulders at its base a savage torrent boiled and foamed. Except for a few places where the rock had crumbled, the ravine's far side was sheer—even if he could cross the torrent, Wandor knew, his enemies would come out on the edge of the ravine before he could climb the wall, and he would be picked off like a target in an archery match, spread-eagled against the rock.

He looked back up the way he had descended, and cautiously flexed his limbs. Pain shot up his left leg. Perhaps he could stay down here, escape notice entirely? He looked up, and as he did, the bushes along the edge of the ravine fifty yards downstream parted and a man stepped out. Tall, blond, a short beard, a rough brown cloak over hacked cuirass, iron cap slung from a broad belt. One of Cragor's men.

Wandor reached for his bow, flexed it twice. He stood up, biting back a gasp at the pain from his knee, pulled an arrow from his quiver, nocked it to the bow. As Wandor stepped out to get a clear shot, the man on the edge looked down, and, as the arrow came flashing up toward him, his mouth opened in a yell.

The yell was cut short as the arrow suddenly sprouted in the man's throat. He reeled backward, clawed at the air, and toppled over the edge of the ravine into the water below. His body had vanished from sight before the sound of the splash died.

From above, there sounded shouts and the thud of feet. Wandor sprang at the bushes. If he could climb the sides of the ravine, he might at least die like a fighting man, instead of like an animal in a trap. He clawed his way up, using arms and his good leg in a frenzy, breath rasping through sealed teeth. He pulled himself up the last few feet, rolled up on to the forest floor, staggered to his feet—

9

and saw three men burst out from behind the trees toward him.

One of them died two seconds later as one of Wandor's throwing knives suddenly blossomed an inch above the neck of his cuirass. The other two stopped and began to circle warily, eyes on Wandor's face—and occasionally shifting their gaze to the Master's emblem swinging against Wandor's heaving chest. Wandor watched them, not daring to take even the few seconds of inattention needed to reach the other throwing knife. He saw a glance flicker between the men facing him. Then they leaped forward together.

One came in high, sword singing hard at the full reach of his arm for Wandor's head. The other sprang in half-crouched, his long dagger lunging upward. Wandor pivoted on his right leg, twisting so that the sword slashed down along his left arm, slicing through the leather sleeve from shoulder to elbow but missing skin and flesh. He flung himself backward, as he did so lashing out with his right foot at the dagger-man's hand. The dagger flew clear and the dagger-man sprawled forward, as Wandor's hand chopped down on the back of his neck.

Now the swordsman had recovered; Wandor drew his own sword, dropped down on to his left knee, and went to the guard position. His opponent charged in. Steel blades clanged and sparked against one another; Wandor parried two clumsy strokes and slashed through his opponent's guard into the man's thigh. He reeled back, then hurled himself forward with his sword held out lance-straight in front of him.

Wandor twisted his head, and the blade seared past his cheek and opened one ear. His own shoulder jerked, his own blade flicked out—and vanished into the other's chest.

Wandor jerked his blade free and snatched the throwing knife from the throat of his first victim, thrusting it still bloody and wet into his belt. Then he staggered to his feet and headed for the trees.

He was barely beyond them when an arrow thunked into a tree, inches from his ear. He nocked an arrow to his own bow and looked through the leaves. A slightly darker patch in the now-twilit woods, a slight movement among the branches, and then his own arrow darted across the clearing and brought a thrashing, struggling figure to the ground. His lips soundlessly formed the word "Five."

Then he was off again, heading toward the cliff. He

could not escape, except to the Hill People (if that could be called escaping), but he could force Cragor's bravos to match their wits with his in the darkness. A good company of them would be his escort on the journey to the Halls of Staz.

By the time he reached the cliff's base it was almost totally dark, with only a faint salmon-hued glow in the western sky. His eyes were now completely adjusted to the dark, and he stared up the cliff. A way up, perhaps? None that he could see, certainly none for a man to mount at night with a lame knee. And at the top, what but death at the hands of the Hill People, death without a warrior's dignity?

The sounds of pursuit had faded. Wandor listened to the night sounds of the forest and wondered at this fact. If his pursuers were fools enough not to realize where they were, the Hill People would have many intruders to deal with this night, instead of one. Yet perhaps the men out there feared the real horrors of Duke Cragor more than the legendary ones of the Hill People? Wandor had heard stories which made this seem possible, and if true, his pursuers would soon resume the trail.

Abruptly there was movement and sound. And there was also light, flickering through the trees in a dozen places, swelling even as Wandor's eyes widened in amazement. The leaves rustled in a suddenly stirred breeze, and the smell of smoke floated up to his nostrils.

He gave a gasp of pure horror. Fire! They had set the woods on fire to burn him out like vermin in a woodpile or rats in a plague-infested city. The tinder-dry summer forest, its floor carpeted with resin-heavy brush and dry needles, would be a sheet of flame within minutes and the wind would drive it up toward the cliff—up toward him.

By the growing light of the flames he limped along the cliff face, looking desperately for a cave or crevice where he might manage some shelter. No great hope of that, and even if he found one—the smoke and the heat would make an end of him just the same, in hardly less time than the flames themselves. He stopped and turned back to face the fire.

It was growing with a speed beyond belief. Flames streamed toward him from the tops of trees, and the growl and roar of the fire now hammered down all other sounds. Already the wind was quickening further, as the hot air from the fire flowed up the hill, smoke bellowing

11

thicker and thicker. Sweat slimed his brow; he uncorked his water bottle and drank. He wiped his face, and his hand came away gray with ashes and soot. Brands and embers whirled toward him; some stung his cheeks. A great branch plummeted out of the smoke, landing within feet of him. He swallowed—the smoke was clawing at his throat.

Then thunder drowning out the fire slammed down from the sky across rocks and trees and flames. A wind from nowhere boiled over the edge of the cliff and whipped the smoke away, revealing a sky no longer black but pulsing with blue and green and purple, monstrous and glowing. The wind increased, and now Wandor saw the flames leap and whirl and flow—and go streaming away toward the road, toward his pursuers. Still the wind increased. Fire-weakened trees split and crashed down; smaller trees and bushes pulled free of the ground entirely and vanished in the howling night. Boulders the size of a man's head and branches as long as a man's body flew through the air as though flung from siege engines.

The light in the sky faded. As though someone had shut a door, the wind died. A moment of utter silence, broken only by the faint crackling of distant and dying flames—and then the rain came. The sky went black and the air went liquid with a sheet of water crashing down on to the forest and the fire. A moment of furious hissing, then no sound except for the rain roaring down, boiling along fresh-cut channels in the ground, sweeping away the last traces of the fire.

Wandor watched it—wounded, exhausted, scorched by the fire, half-strangled by the smoke, flogged raw by the wind, and now half-drowned in the rain. Then he sank numbly into the mud and tried to shelter his face with his hands.

With a suddenness that was now no surprise, the rain ceased. The night was quiet again. Water ran down Wandor's face and hands, and dripped softly into the mud that clung around his feet. A faint crash floated up on the breeze as a last tree collapsed.

Wandor looked up. Nothing was moving in the forest. And he was safe—battered, but safe. He did not know how or why or by whom he had been saved, but his curiosity in these matters was not so great that he thought it worth staying within a mile of the Hill People's legendary dark shrine long enough to find out. He rose to his feet, checked his gear, and started back down the hill.

This time, it happened slowly. A faint glow suddenly crept over the landscape, wavered for a moment, then slowly and steadily brightened. No savage glare of the fire, but rather a peaceful, gentle, gold-tinged luminosity. Behind him, Wandor heard the sound of grinding rock, then a sudden silence.

He turned and saw them. Five of them—small square figures silhouetted against the golden glow pouring from a high, wide opening where Wandor had before seen only solid rock. They stood in silence, motionless, neither threatening nor beckoning.

Wandor tightened the straps of his blanket roll, and again examined his weapons. Then he brushed the mud off his breeches and started back up the hill.

II

THE FIVE FIGURES remained motionless as Wandor approached them. As he did so, his coiling nameless lurking fears of hill-dwelling demons fled into the darkness. These stocky little men with their broad, dark-brown faces and close-curling dark hair were like those he had seen all his life around Trorim, carting wood and water, peddling vegetables and eggs at the market—and darting in frantic terror from the paths of the high, proud horses of the gentry and the nobles. He spread his hands apart in the gesture of peace, and stepped forward.

They looked at him in silence until he was almost to them, then the one farthest forward spoke.

"Greetings, lowlander. Come with us. You will be fed and bathed and your wounds attended. Then the Elders will sit in judgment, and you will be dealt with as they judge you to deserve."

Wandor stiffened at the last words. The leader noticed this, and seemed to smile.

"Come. We have suffered much from your people, so our laws are harsh toward those who come among us from the lowlands. Yet we are not as the beasts of the forests; we have a Law, and each man receives proper judgment under it." He turned and beckoned toward the mouth of the cave. Without a word, Wandor stepped inside. The five Hill People followed, and with the same grinding of rock a great stone slid across the opening behind them.

The passage wound steadily downward, sometimes at a gentle slope, sometimes so steeply that the floor became a flight of broad steps, carved out of the rock and edged and faced with bright-yellow brick. The golden light filling the passage came, it seemed, from crystal globes mounted in massive polished-wood brackets set in the walls and filled with some granular paste that gave off an unwavering glow. Again, the leader of the little group noticed Wandor's gaze wandering to the lights, and was quick with an explanation.

"The crystal is from our own mines, here in the great mountains. That inside is a moss we gather by night in the forests, and treat according to a formula even older than our people." Wandor shuddered slightly, trying to imagine the origins of something older than these squat brown people who had held all the land of Benzos and even to the north, when the Hond came out of the west so many years ago that even this was swallowed up in legends. But he held his peace. The fewer of their secrets he knew, the more willing the Hill People might be to let him go free.

After what may have been anything from minutes to hours, the six men came to a great iron-bound double door. The leader stepped up to a small hole in the rock wall and spoke into it.

"Dagolk and his Four, with a lowlander intruder."

There was a clanking and a creaking within, and the great doors swung open.

They stepped through the door and on to a wooden balcony which ran around a vast gold-lit cavern near its domed roof. From both the sand-strewn floor far below and the balcony itself, other passages and doors opened off, and it was through one of these doors they led Wandor. He found himself in a small chamber with a pallet of leather stuffed with pine needles, a rough table and stool, a blanket sewn together from the skins of mountain sheep, and in the corner a small basin through which water from a cleft in the rock gurgled steadily. There they left him.

Soon two women and a boy appeared; they bound his wounds with leaves and smeared his cuts and burns and bruises with a strong-smelling green salve. Then they fed him thick hot soup, a great wooden platter of roasted nuts ground and mixed with smoked boar's meat, cheese and onions, and a tall leather cup of acorn beer. His own clothes and gear were piled neatly in a corner and covered with an animal hide, then one woman and the boy slipped out and the other woman sat back against the wall by the door and looked at him while he ate.

15

Woman? Girl, rather, for she could hardly have been more than fourteen or fifteen. Wandor found this cheered him considerably. In his experience of the rougher side of the world, which was fairly extensive, fourteen-year-old girls were seldom given charge of desperate and dangerous prisoners. Perhaps their intentions toward him were less than totally murderous; perhaps, on the other hand, the meal had been simply the ample meal that even barbarians were said to give the condemned. Did the girl know anything about his prospective fate? No harm in asking, at any rate. . . .

"Why did you feed me so well?" The girl jumped slightly, looked sharply at him, pulled her dark hair across her face while she considered, and then answered with a smile.

"Because you were fleeing from the Black Duke's men, who put fire to the trees of Mother Yeza and brought death among the things of the forest. We give help to the Black Duke's enemies whenever we can, for he is our enemy above all others."

"The Black Duke? Duke Cragor?"

"Yes. Although I do not know why *you* were fleeing him, for he is no enemy to the lowlanders, but leads them against us to kill and burn and steal."

Wandor laughed. He'd better lay this girl's suspicions to rest now, and also teach her a few of the truths of life outside her native hills. "Cragor does that on occasion, to be sure, but go down into the lowlands and ask when you are sure no one else will overhear, and you will find a host of people who would gladly see Duke Cragor roasted alive over a slow fire. Few love him, except those he has bought, or the great nobles and their retainers, who hope he will bring back the good old days when they ruled all the lands of Benzos, each according to his own whim, and the king was nothing."

The girl shuddered. "And then nothing will be safe in the hills. What little justice we have had from the lowlanders, it has come from their kings." She was silent for a moment, then looked at him again closely. "Are you truly a lowlander—truly a Hond? I have heard the stories of them, and they are all said to be tall and blond and slender and pale-faced. You are tall, but your hair is as black as ours and your skin not much lighter."

Wandor sighed. "I know. When I was an apprentice of the Order of Duelists, most of my personal duels were with ill-mannered fellows who called me a woodland rootgrubber, or some such name. But they may have been right, when I think it over.

"You see, I was a foundling child. I was raised by a goldsmith of Trorim and his wife, but they said they found me under some bushes beside a field along the western fringe of your Hills, with the body of a woman they thought was my true mother—tall, but colored like the Sthi of the Hills, and with a rich grayfox robe and gold necklace. She had been stabbed many times, but she dragged herself and me into hiding before she died."

"And you remember nothing of that woman?"

"No—it was twenty-five years ago, and they reckoned I was at most three years old. I speak the tongue of the Sthi as I do because my 'father' was—is—a wealthy man, and had me reared by a nurse of those people." He shook his head. "No, the only thing I have from my true mother is an ornament that was found in a leather bag near where she lay. No doubt her killers dropped it in their flight. A strange thing, too: a crystal pyramid, about the size of my fist, with a tiny gold chair at the top, and mounted on a piece of metal so hard that none of my father's acids could touch it, and covered with inscriptions like——"

The girl's face turned pasty white and her hands crept slowly up to her face and jammed into her mouth. Her eyes turned to vast empty black pools, her whole body began to quiver, and Wandor heard her saying softly, "Oh, Mother Yeza, Mother Yeza, Mother Yeza!" her voice rising slowly to a shriek. Then she sprang to her feet and panther-quick leaped through the door. Several dark faces peered after her, then turned their gaze inward, to where Wandor sat in amazement on his pallet. Amazement and the beginnings of fear. What deadly secret of these grim and dark people had he stumbled on *now*?

Feet shuffled in the corridor, and a murmuring arose, to be cut off abruptly in a great united gasp. Then through the door came the girl, leading an old woman. Old? The brown skin, faded and crinkled like ancient parchment, stretched over a narrow frame of bones moving so slowly Wandor fancied he could hear the rusty creaking and squealing of joints. Bare brown feet, a scalp bare but for a fringe of pale hair, eyes—and Wandor's stomach went cold again when he saw those eyes. The old woman's eyes were beyond the seeing of everyday things, beyond the seeing of men's bodies, fit only to look into their souls and drag them quivering out into the light. He looked across

17

the room to where his weapons were piled. No, there was no mortal weapon, and no skill in wielding it, that could help him now.

She spoke. *"Vryulom serdca oiklom grasdit?"*

Wandor felt the words tugging faintly at something deep within his mind, but they awakened no memories and no understanding of their meaning. He shook his head and spread his hands in a placating gesture. She repeated the question. Again, he had to remain silent. She looked sharply at him, then sighed faintly. "I asked too much. If it is in him, why after all these years should it be in his waking mind? If it is in him, we must bring it out from deep within his soul." She turned to the girl. "Bring the Dark Water." The girl darted out.

After what seemed like hours, she returned, carrying a small bronze ewer and a smaller crystal cup rimmed with gold. The old woman took the ewer and poured its contents into the cup—a dark blue-black liquid that bubbled and smoked and gave off an acrid, moldy stench. She thrust the cup at Wandor. "Drink!"

It tasted even worse than it smelled. He sat while it went down and his stomach heaved and shuddered. The faces surrounding him took on an air of watchfulness.

Then it seemed that in a moment the faces and the light and the cave walls and everything in the cave were snatched away to a vast distance. Small . . . smaller . . . gone! And Wandor was alone on a shimmering black plain under a searing bright silver sky where glowing red masses swept past overhead in a howling wind. . . .

Gone! And he was standing knee-deep in waving purple grass with the same wind roaring through a forest of great stately trees, tossing heart-shaped leaves the size of a man in a wild dance. Rain slashed through the canopy of trees into his face; his black hair streamed from his head, spread fan-wise in the gale. . . .

Gone! And there was utter blackness all around him, broken only by a mighty pillar of golden fire that shot up before him, then collapsed into a pulsing seething lake of fire where monstrous shadow-figures danced and flickered. . . .

Gone! And he was back in the cave beneath Mount Pendwyr, lying on the pallet with a dozen anxious faces bent over him. The old woman—he somehow knew now that she was Kayopla, High Priestess of Mother Yeza—pushed her face close to his and repeated her question.

18

Now somehow it seemed fitting, somehow he was not surprised; it was no meaningless gabble, but a simple, ordinary question. "Do you understand me?"

Wandor forced his tongue and lips to shape sounds in the same language. "Yes, I understand you."

The old woman's eyes blazed open, and all around him the watchers sucked in their breaths. Kayopla bent over him again, and said sharply, "What did Mother Yeza show you? Describe it!"

He did so. The plain, the forest, the golden pillar in the blackness—and when he came to that Kayopla and all the watchers around him cried out aloud and fell prone on the rock floor, pressing their foreheads against the rock while their lips moved frantically in an outpouring of soundless prayers. They were not worshiping him, they were not worshiping any god or goddess or spirit that Wandor had heard of—but the prayers poured out and Wandor licked dry lips and swallowed and watched them.

Finally the Sthi rose to their feet, and Kayopla made a sharp beckoning gesture. Four men in green robes girdled with silver chains advanced through the crowd into the room, and stepped up to Wandor. "Rise!" hissed Kayopla.

Wandor rose. The four men looked at him, and then at one another, and finally one of them—the same Dagolk who had guided him into the caves from the forest outside—spoke:

"Bertan Wandor. You came to us in flight from the Black Duke, and from men who laid impious fire to the woods of Mother Yeza. For this the spirits of the Hills were called, and by them was sent the storm to save you and slay those who were alike your enemies and ours. And for this we have received you as a friend and given you food and healing.

"But you may be more than you seem. By the story of your life, by the royal pendant you possess, and, above all, by the knowledge of the Kingly Tongue of the Sthi brought out of you by the Dark Waters, you seem to be of the Kingly Race of the Sthi. If this be so, you are the rightful heir to the High Throne of the hills.

"And you may be still more than this. In the Ancient Days, there was a king of the blood of the Sthi, and he wore Five Crowns and all the world owed him homage and lived at peace with one another. Then the Years of Darkness came upon us, and men became as beasts, and the world we know today came into being. But from those days to this there has been among us—and among those who honor and guard the wisdom of the Ancient Days—a prophecy, that a King shall once more rise from the Kingly House of the Sthi, to wear the Five Crowns and bring men to peace."

Dagolk swallowed. "The vision of the golden pillar is sent by Mother Yeza to those who are to be brought before the Mountain Voice, who alone can recognize the Five-Crowned King. Bertan Wandor, we have come to take you before the Mountain Voice, there to be judged and tested and to give your fate entirely into its hands. Do you consent?"

Wandor's head was whirling even more than the Dark Waters should have caused. His voice, when he finally summoned it up, was a croak. "I do."

III

DAGOLK MOTIONED him toward the door. "Then follow us. We will take you to the Royal Boat, and it will take you before the Voice."

Wandor followed the four men out of the little cave. As he fell into step behind them, two strong men lifted Kayopla into the seat of a litter—lifted her and the litter and trotted after them. The little procession moved quickly along the balcony, heads popping out of curtained doorways and then vanishing hastily as they passed, until they came to a door set in the wall—a door of solid rock set with mystic signs worked in rubies and bolted with a bronze bar thick as a man's calf and sculptured in the form of a serpent. Two sentries stood before it, armed with hide shields and short swords; Dagolk spoke to them and they stood aside. The door slid aside with a rumble and a rasp, revealing a long corridor stretching away into shadow. Dagolk took down one of the crystal lamps from the wall and stepped forward; the rest followed.

For the first minutes, Wandor followed like a man dazed. His fear of being marched to his death, not merely without honor but out of sight of any living human being, returned. He uttered a short prayer to Staz the Warrior that he might not die without facing at least one human foe that he could meet and take with him. He had no weapons but what nature gave him; still, a trained Master of the Order was held equal to any three ordinary men though he faced them as naked as the day of his birth. But for this his mind must be clear. To order his mind, and drive fear from it, Wandor began to count his steps, to judge the length of his journey.

He had counted five hundred and ninety paces when abruptly the close-pressing walls and ceiling of rough-hewn rock vanished, and the golden light of the lantern shone pitifully small in a huge vaulted chamber of fitted stone. Wandor could see that some of the nacreous slabs were the size of a peasant's cottage, yet they butted on one another with gaps through which the thinnest knife blade could barely have been thrust. Here and there in the walls loomed massive doorways, the stone doors twice the height of a man hung in intricately carved frames.

Two hundred paces farther on, the roof vanished entirely; the lantern's rays were lost entirely in a vast black immensity. Before them a flight of stairs plunged down into blackness, a flight of stairs wide enough for a troop of cavalry to descend abreast—its edges were barely visible as dim gray bulks of masonry at the very edge of vision.

For an immeasurable time they descended the stairs into the depths, and Wandor found that he had at last succeeded in driving fear out of his mind. The gods would give him dignity at his death, whatever men or the demons they might call up as allies could do. And there was nothing else left to fear. Moreover, he was becoming fascinated by what surrounded him. The horrible tales of the Hill People's rites spoke of caverns and voices, to be sure, but nothing like this—a vast maze of stone that might be the cellar of some inconceivably huge royal palace, but yet seemed too vast even for that. And the legend of the Five-Crowned King—a legend, it seemed, in which he was being called on to play a part. He quickened his pace until he was abreast of Dagolk, and spoke softly to him. "What is the Mountain Voice to whom I am being taken?"

Dagolk jumped at the sound, then recovered and replied.

"It dwells in the fire beneath Mount Pendwyr, the fire in the center of the Lake of Night. It is neither god nor man nor demon, nor anything for which we have words, although it takes the form of a man when it speaks to us. It always speaks in the Kingly Tongue of the Sthi, which the High Priestess of Yeza learns in her youth, but which the Kingly House carries in its soul—as do you.

"Some parts of the legend of the Five-Crowned King tell of the last wearer of the Five Crowns, who, when he felt his end near, had himself borne down through the tunnels built by his House and cast into the flames. The flames took his spirit and kept it alive, and from within the flames he watches over the world and speaks to the Kingly House of the Sthi. He watches, and guards, and waits for the Five-Crowned Kings to come again and bring his Guardianship to an end."

Wandor shuddered. "And these tunnels and rooms and steps—the Five-Crowned Kings built them?"

"They—or some powers they could call up. The Kings of the Years of Darkness and since have neither the gold nor the magic to carve palaces and halls out of the living rock of our mountains."

Minutes later they reached the bottom of the stairs, and the lanternlight revealed a vast expanse of inky water, stretching off into the darkness, and lapping gently at a short stone quay at their feet. Beside the quay rode a small skiff, high-prowed and carvel-planked, with a single carved seat in the stern and elongated bird and beast figures etched in gold along the thwarts. Dagolk pointed toward the boat and said to Wandor: "There is the Royal Boat. Once it took the Five-Crowned Kings up and down the rivers of their Kingdoms. Now it will take you of its own accord to the Fire in the center of the lake. You cannot see it from here; it is concealed and contained within a great rock shaft, with only one opening which the boat will seek out. Enter the boat, and may Mother Yeza and all Her spirits have you in their keeping."

Wandor climbed in and settled himself in the seat. The boat sat motionless for a moment, then rocked sharply, swung its prow away from the quay and swept away into the darkness so fast that spray from the bow arched into the air and dampened Wandor's face. In less than a minute, the lantern on the quay sank to a distant glow like summer fireflies; in a few seconds more it was utterly gone. Wandor was alone in the darkness with only the sound of the rushing water at the prow of the boat.

How long the boat rushed across the well-named Lake of Night, Wandor had no idea. Nor had he any idea of his direction. But gradually he felt the boat heeling into a wide turn, and the rush of water slackened. A moment later the boat stopped entirely, then began to move forward again, slowly—and suddenly the darkness ahead was split from the water to some unguessable height by a great golden column, pouring out a pulsing, flickering light like the door of an open forge.

As he approached, Wandor saw this appearance was no accident—the column was actually a cleft as high as a temple's tower in a great rock wall, curving away into the darkness on either side of solid and impenetrable as the mountain itself but for the one opening. Through this opening the boat slid quietly, with a faint lapping of water at its bow.

Beyond the cleft, the water opened out again into a vast gilded pool that rippled against the edges of an immense circular chamber, half a mile across and rising at least as high above the water. In the center of the pool stood a steep cone of jagged blue-black rock, rising two hundred feet above the water. It was from the broad top of this cone that the light was pouring. On one side of the cone, a flight of steps led down from the top to the water, and it was at the foot of these steps that the boat came to rest.

Wandor climbed out, tightened the belt of his robe, took several deep breaths, and began to climb. The steps were high and steep, and he needed all those breaths by the time he stood on the top step and gazed out at the view.

The top of the cone was a pit, three hundred feet broad, with vertical sides plummeting down to the unimaginably great depth below where the golden fire swirled and leaped. Halfway around the rim of the pit, a great stone lintel was cantilevered out over the fire below. And on its outermost end . . . Wandor stopped and gasped in amazement.

Out there, thrust into space above the fire here far below Mount Pendwyr, was the same ornament his "parents" had found near him in the woods twenty-five years ago— duplicated in every minute detail, but fifty—a hundred— times as large. The crystal pyramid was twice the height of a man, the golden chair was man-sized and covered with serpentine runes picked out with precious stones and more slabs of crystal and opal and jade, the seat covered with a purple cushion bordered in silver cloth. Wandor stood in silence and bewilderment and some fear, until a distant but distinct prompting in his mind said clearly to him: "Go and mount the Seat of the Kings."

As he sank into the purple cushion and leaned back, the flames far below sank into momentary quiescence. Then they poured up from the depths in a whirling, searing sheet, filling the pit with fire and the vast cavern with a still-brighter light. All around Wandor the flames hurled themselves into the air, spurted over the edge of the pit, twisted themselves for moments into human shapes, roared and screamed and flared—and did not burn.

As Wandor sat there unharmed amid the flames, he

saw the light change, from gold to crimson, and far down in the firepit a solid crimson shape began to coalesce out of the flames, rising as it did so. It rose level with his eyes, hung in the air—jerked, twisted, writhed—then flowed smoothly into human shape.

It hung there above the fire now, a tall bronze-skinned man, his long hair and beard shimmering blue black in the light, naked except for a small cap of bright metal and a great necklace from which hung five small jeweled golden crowns. With regal grace, the man raised a long muscular arm in the salute of honor.

"Greetings and honor, man. What is your name in the world of men, and why come you here to me, the Guardian of the Mountain?"

"My name is Bertan Wandor. I have come to you for a testing, to know whether I am the man of the Kingly House of the Sthi destined one day to wear the Five Crowns of the Ancient Days."

The form flickered back to shapeless crimson for an eye-blink, then was steady in human shape again. "So the dream yet lives. Good. As men reckon time, it has been a hundred years since Mother Yeza sent the vision to a man and called him to me."

"The dream?" Wandor's tone reflected the blankness of his mind.

"The dream of peace and brotherhood under one law!" The great voice sounded impatient, like an elderly teacher asked to explain the obvious. "Men still dream of it and strive toward it, though it has been nothing real since the men of my fathers' House walked the living world and their bodies dwelt in the halls of the Five-Crowned Kings and sent forth their laws and their armies over the lands and their peoples."

Wandor stared. So the legend of the last of the Five-Crowned Kings had some truth in it. But testing the truth of ancient legends was not his business here. He began again. "I have come here for a testing——"

"*Here* there is no testing for you!" and on "here!" the great voice rose to a thunderblast that whirled the flames like a gale of wind and rang from all the surrounding rocks. "He who would rule all the world of men, there must he be tested. *Go!* Go, and of what I say to you, speak not one word except to those who shall be part of your testing.

"Go and win Firehair the Maiden.

"Go and win the faith of Strong-Ax and Fear-No-Devil.

"Go and win aid from Cheloth of the Woods.

"Go and seek these—the Helm of Jagnar, the Ax of Yevoda, the Spear of Valkath, the Sword of Artos, the Dragon-Steed of Morkol.

"Go among all peoples and through all lands and against all who torment and distress men, wherever you find them barring your passage.

"Go then to the house of him you call father and take up the talisman and watch, while Mount Pendwyr splits with fire and the hills and woods rise into the sky and are scattered to the sea.

"Go then at last forth to battle, and smite those who come against you, with all your strength and cunning.

"All such will be your testing. The road is long. The testing is great. May your strength be great also."

Silence again. The great form raised its hand in salute again, then flowed and flickered and was once more flame. And the flames themselves sank back down the pit as fast as they had risen. Wandor was alone again on the golden chair.

He remembered rising and stumbling back to the head of the stairs, but nothing after that until he found himself lying on his pallet in the little cave, with Kayopla pressing a sponge dampened with some sweet-scented liquor against his lips and the girl rubbing his cold and bloodless hands. Dagolk stood by the door; as Wandor stirred and looked about him, the man's face broke into a faint smile.

"You have returned to us in mind as well as body, praise the Mother. We had begun to fear the Guardian had sent back an empty shell of flesh, fit only for burying."

Wandor shook his head painfully.

"Good. Can you tell us any thing of what passed there, by the Fire?" Kayopla looked sharply at him, then at Wandor, who, remembering how his head hurt, simply said "No."

"I feared as much. The Guardian's purposes are revealed to one man at a time, it would seem."

He sighed, then said briskly: "The Guardian has dealt with you, and bound you to silence. From this it would seem that you must do what is bidden you out in the world, away from our caves and hills, and our duty is thus to set you on your way. This we will do, as soon as you feel that you can mount a horse and ride. You will have the pick of our stables and food and drink for your journey."

"Enough to spare me the need to stop at inns on my way?"

"If you desire."

"I do. Duke Cragor, or whoever sent the band after me, may believe I perished in the fire or the storm as long as I am not seen alive. If I can get to Benzor unheralded, so much the better."

"Indeed. And you need not fear anything in our woods or hills, so you can ride by night if you wish. The Sthi of the hills and all who obey their law are henceforward your friends and allies and servants in whatever you may undertake."

IV

THE ROYAL CAPITAL of Benzor held some two hundred and fifty thousand of the twenty million subjects of the Kings of Benzos. As Wandor rode up the Great West Road toward the city wall, it seemed that all of them were on the move at once this morning.

It was a typical morning of early summer in the capital —a fast-fading coolness in an air that held ample promise of the stifling, baking heat of the afternoon, and also the reek of middens, slops, pigs, and the great River Avar. The markets were in full session, and all the roads and streets cutting through the buildings beyond the wall were choked with high-piled farm carts, wheelbarrows, the pack horses and mules of merchant caravans, and even strings of laden camels from the far south, with their brass-laden Chonga harnesses.

In the four days since he had ridden away from Mount Pendwyr, Wandor had learned to trust the little hill mare's judgment and sureness of foot, and so let her pick her own path through the dust and the din. A hundred paces from the high-towered, flag-crowned West Gate, traffic slowed to a complete halt. A look ahead revealed a four-wheeled cart laden with wine barrels tipped on its side across the road, with a storm of curses and blasphemies and grunts of effort swirling around it, as a dozen men struggled to set it upright again.

Wandor gave up, turned the mare's head to the left, and headed for the Ferry Road leading down to the Avar. It took him a mile around the circuit of the great wall. As he rode, his eyes picked out the glint of helmets and armor on the walk, and occasionally a stern face peering through the crenelation to look down on the road and the hovels that squatted in their own filth on either side of it.

The ferryman was doing a full business of men and loads, and it seemed to Wandor that among the men more than usual were wearing armor and carried well-worn weapons, slung ready for instant use. There were men in the green and silver of the royal Household Troops of King Nond, the peacock hues of half-a-dozen great lords, the sober black of the civic guard, and no small number in the gray cloaks of unattached mercenaries. However, no amount of business will stay a ferryman's tongue, and this one was no exception.

"Morning, sir," he said, sweeping Wandor's coins into his leather purse. "And what might your doings be today?"

"I've come in from the west for hiring out as a mercenary, if there's any such work to be found," replied Wandor. There was no hope of hiding all of his profession—not with sword and bow riding in open sight.

"Well, and you'll not be looking far, that I may tell you. Every noble in the land from the Duke Cragor himself on down, and every merchant house and shopkeeper, is looking for men sharp with a sword or bow and dagger, and if you come to them with a horse besides. . . ." He made a name-your-own-price gesture.

More passengers flooded aboard, and soon the ferryman was able to step to the stern and cast off. The great horse-driven windlass on the far bank began to creak, arm-thick animal hide ropes tightened with a chorus of groans, and the ferry moved out across the crowded Avar.

They were two thirds of the way across the mile-wide stream when Wandor raised his eyes from contemplating a passing raft of logs, with a family of six clustered around a small stone hearth on its stern, to see smoke pouring up, thick and gray, from the far bank of the river. He shaded his eyes against the sun-glaring water and looked again.

Curses and damnation! The smoke was billowing up from the Khindi quarter—another pogrom, the gods help those poor wretches. And Wandor saw his hopes of reaching Benzor unheralded and unknown going up in that same rising smoke, for, of all the Rules of the Order of Duelists, none was more sacred than the Seventh:

Rule the Seventh: Whensoever there be the weak and helpless oppressed by lawless violence, it shall be the duty of all members and apprentices of the Order to bring their strength and weaponscraft to assist them, while remaining true to all the other Rules of the Order in so doing.

In plain language, this meant that if a House Master such as Wandor saw a maiden in distress, he had to go to her assistance at once, wearing his House Master's emblem openly on his chest. Which was not the most pleasant prospect when one's life might depend on concealing one's identity.

However, the rule was not to be winked at. Wandor cursed bitterly as he checked his weapons and tightened the saddle girth, calling down the wrath of Staz the Warrior and Alfod the Judge on whoever had started the pogrom. But when the ferry ramp rattled down and squashed into the mud of the bank, he was mounted and armed. The moment the path ahead cleared, he spurred the mare to a gallop, charging up the road and scattering children and chickens before him.

The scene when he reached the mud-brick and shagbark log wall around the Khindi quarter was the usual one of the pogrom—a third of the huts ablaze, a third standing gape-windowed while looters boiled in and out with armfuls of chairs and curtains and ragged linens and cracked wooden bowls to pile on the bonfires flaming in the middle of the mud streets, the last third closed tight while looters hammered at locked doors and windows and screams sounded from inside.

The nearest hut was of the third group; Wandor drew his sword and spurred toward the four half-naked men who were swinging sledges against the door. They wheeled at his approach, raising their hammers—and around the corner of the hut burst a screaming Khindi girl, clutching the remaining rags of her dress to her body, while two men clumped heavily after her.

The Duelist sword was not ideally suited for work on horseback, but, swung by a strong and angry and skilled Duelist, it would serve. The two lust-blinded men charged straight into Wandor's reach, and five seconds later they both lay in the mud, one's throat gaping from ear to ear, that other's head completely severed from his trunk. The other four men charged in toward Wandor. One reached for the mare's bridle, and had the reaching arm hacked off at the shoulder, but as he fell screaming into the mud, one of his fellows swung at the mare's head and Wandor heard the skull crunch and felt the stricken beast begin to topple sideways.

He landed on his feet and made the horse-killer pay for his victory with four inches of sword blade rammed between his ribs. The two survivors sprang hastily out of his reach, but other figures now were emerging from the smoke and charging in toward him, with hammers and axes and long saw-edged daggers. He dropped two of them with his throwing knives, then set his back against the cottage wall and went to work on the forest of darting limbs and waving heads and trunks before him, taking small wounds, giving mortal ones, thrusting and parrying and weaving and darting and——

Hooves thundered in his ears and the forest before him suddenly dissolved into a mass of frantic men, scattering in all directions as a squadron of the Household Cavalry came sweeping in, lances waving high before dipping to their work. One cavalry trooper went down with an arrow through his thigh, then the whole battle vanished in the murk amid footfalls and hoofbeats and war yells and death screams. . . .

Wandor was binding up the last of his wounds when a tall horseman in cuirass and open-faced helm, with the badge of the Order of Knights clanking on his armored chest, rode out of the thinning smoke and spoke to him.

"Good work, my man," he said, then, noticing Wandor's emblem: "Your pardon, House Master."

"Nothing to pardon, sir," replied Wandor. "And what I did, I did as my duty."

"If all of King Nond's subjects did their duty as well, it would be a better kingdom," said the officer with a sigh. "This is the fifth such in the past year, and every time we have to cut down the dirty wretches whom Cragor buys to do this, people scream against the horrors of Nond's oppression." He spat savagely into the mud. "We put a good forty of them under the earth this time, plus the half-dozen odd you took. That should give them pause, the next time some smooth-tongued heavy-pursed swine comes round to rouse them. Might I ask your name?"

Wandor swallowed. "This we do as our duty, as I told you. We are permitted to receive public honors only if permitted by our Grand Master." He knew the speech sounded pompous; he didn't care. He cared only about getting out of this smoke and blood to the quiet of the Duelists' House and the coarse wisdom of the Grand Master.

The officer shrugged. "You Duelists are a stiff-necked lot. They say we Knights are proud, but you people—gods above! Would you at least be willing to borrow one of our horses, since your own seems to be of no further use? Send me a message at the castle barracks when you've finished with it—Count Ferjor of the Tenth Cavalry Regiment."

Wandor considered for a moment, then nodded.

An hour later with the borrowed horse in the skilled hands of the grooms at the House Stables and his own body bathed, bandaged, and clad in a House Master's formal cloak thrown over hastily borrowed tunic and breeches, Wandor was mounting the stairs to the High Chamber of the House and his meeting with the Grand Master. Apprentices and servants sprang from his path with alarmed mutterings and propitiatory gestures. Wandor had heard it said that when he killed, his face wore for hours afterward an expression fit to make demons shudder. Perhaps it was true; he would have to find a mirror.

There was no mirror in the High Chamber, nor was there any Grand Master—both the Seat of Honor and the Chamber were empty, except for two apprentices kneeling before the shrine of Staz. The portraits of the Five Heroes of the Order hung on one wall. Wandor went down on his knees before them and recited the Formula of Honor with rather more fervor than usual:

"Jilgath Strongbow, Eprim Blackblade, Hafnor of Tafardos, Màster Nikor, Master Bleckor of the Knives, by Staz the Warrior this I swear, to hold you in honor, to take from your deeds the model of my own, to take from your courage the source of my own, to take from your deaths the manner of my own."

He rose and turned—and faced the Grand Master.

The Grand Master was in his undress robe, and his red face, with its long thick nose and bristling white mustache, peered out from under his ordinary velvet cap, rather than the ceremonial gold helm. He did not speak, but only made a beckoning gesture to Wandor.

The Grand Master led Wandor across the Hall past the Shrine of Staz, through a curtained doorway, up a short flight of stairs, and into his private chamber set in the outer wall of the House. The chamber was bare, except for a brilliant tapestry on one wall, showing the Hero Eprim Blackblade in his single-handed death duel against the twelve mercenary swordsmen of Baron Gostor, a bench, a battered oak table, and two chairs. The Grand Master seated himself in one, motioned Wandor to the other, and rang for wine. When it had appeared, and they had drunk the ritual toasts and one or two personal ones, the Grand Master set down his cup and looked sharply at Wandor.

"You are somewhat late, Master Wandor. We expected you two days ago."

"I was delayed in the Hills." The Grand Master's eyebrows climbed upward until they were lost under the brim of his cap. Wandor sighed faintly, then emptied his own cup, refilled it from the bronze bowl and told a suitably edited version of his journey.

When he had finished, the Grand Master took off his cap, looked Wandor up and down, drained off another cup of wine, and said, "I have served the Order fifty years, and so I have enough faith in it to believe that one who has risen to House Master in it will tell the truth. Otherwise, I would call your story the most fair-spun fancy I have ever heard, even from the bards at King Nond's court."

Wandor half-rose. "And I, sir, would then be forced to ask satisfaction from you or your appointed champion. I could not——"

The Grand Master's cup banged down on the table with a crash like a falling drawbridge. "Sit down and stop ruffling your feathers, you damned young cockerel! Don't waste your blows on useless old carcasses like mine. Save them for the King's enemies."

He took a deep breath. "You were ordered here at the request of His Sacred Majesty, King Nond II, to be sent as his agent on a secret mission of the greatest importance. Don't gape like that—you look like a fresh-caught apprentice. I don't know a damned thing about this mission, although I have my suspicions. However, the King's description of what he wanted was an almost perfect description of you, so *whatever* it is, you're for it."

Wandor frowned. "How was the description put?"

"'A man of strong and active body and quick mind, fluent speech, handsome in face and expert with as many weapons as possible.' Don't blush like a schoolgirl—I can't, the gods have mercy upon me, escape the fact that you're nearly as good as you think you are. With that, and the help of the gods, you may muddle through whatever the King hands you." He looked at the hourglass. "It's nearly prime. The King's in his best mood after he's eaten and digested a good meal, so if you leave now, you should reach the castle right on time."

"The castle?"

"Yes. Didn't you know? Shows what things have come to, when Benzos's anointed King has to wall himself up in Manga Castle."

V

Two HUNDRED YEARS before, when the Kings of Benzos
were hammering away at the power of their nobles, the
reigning King came to the village of Manga, where the
High Roads from the North and the South met the one
from the East, and ran with it fifteen miles west to Benzor.
And after the King came a thousand soldiers and a thousand workmen and a thousand overseers and ten thousand
slaves and twenty thousand free peasants and four thousand wagonloads of food and beer and tools and clothes
and timber and ironmongery. They came to a hill west of
the village, rising high and rock-faced out of the plain
south of the Avar, and they began to dig and build.

They dug a canal deep enough for tall ships from the
Avar a mile to the base of the hill, and then a moat forty
feet wide and thirty feet deep around the hill itself, a circuit
of three good miles, and filled it from the canal. The earth
from the moat they heaped up twenty feet high with a
vertical slope on the outside, and atop the heap they built
a stone wall twenty feet high and ten feet thick, with towers
every three hundred feet. From the towers stairs ran down
through the mound, through the earth, into the solid rock,
into tunnels leading under the moat. These tunnels were
wide enough for three men to walk abreast, and, if those
in the castle wished, they could open great bronze valves
and flood the tunnels against all comers.

Inside the moat, they carved the sides of the hill into
bare rock walls rising thirty feet above the moat. Atop the
rock they built another stone wall, this one forty feet high
and twenty thick, with more towers along its length.
At the base of one of these towers was a double gate, with

35

an iron portcullis and two great iron doors and a wooden drawbridge wide enough for five mounted men, raised and lowered by a chain with links as thick as a man's arm.

Inside the walls they built a circular keep two hundred feet high and a hundred feet in diameter, with walls of fitted stone twenty-five feet thick at the base, its own well and storerooms and living quarters. They built a Great Hall that measured fifty feet from floor to vault, a chapel to the Five Gods enriched with the craftsmanship of fifty Masters of a dozen Guilds, quarters for the King and his Household, barracks for five thousand men, stables for a thousand horses, lofts and cellars for five hundred women and a thousand servants, smithies and armories and saddlers' shops and a royal mews and a royal kennel. Out of the solid rock they carved two more wells three hundred feet down into the earth, and great heavy-vaulted caves to hold, clean and safe, grain and biscuit, cheese and salt meat, dried fruits and pickled vegetables, beer and wine and spirits for five thousand men for two years, and connected them all with a spiderweb of tunnels.

Between one spring and another, all this rose on the hill near Manga. And from that day, Manga Castle stood and glared at the world, and sheltered the Kings of Benzos in their times of need.

The royal banner of the House of Nobor, green with the silver leopard rampant, was streaming from the keep as Wandor rode up to the gate on the outer edge of the moat. The guards who challenged him were scarred and weather-beaten veterans of the Royal Foot Guard. The King was indeed in residence, and guarding himself closely.

The guards passesd Wandor through, and he rode across the drawbridge, under the double gates with their iron doors slid back into the walls, and left his horse with the grooms at the guest stables. The officer at the door of the keep looked him up and down several times, frowned, then passed him in and relocked the door behind him.

As Wandor climbed up the spiral stairs in the keep wall, he noticed that the door of each floor into the central chambers was guarded by two or even three sentries, with well-polished but dented cuirasses and well-oiled weapons slung ready for instant use. At the very top, the door was closed. He knocked and stated his name and business, an eyehole slipped open, and there was a nervous moment's examination, then the door slid silently open and Wandor entered.

It was a low-ceilinged, narrow antechamber, bare stone except for the lantern hanging from the ceiling and a rack of short spears against one wall. Two guards promptly stepped out of niches in the walls with drawn weapons and grabbed his arms, then released him at the peremptory gesture of the man standing at the far end of the room.

He was a youngish man, though older than Wandor; two or three inches taller but more slender, with sandy hair cut short, a close-trimmed soldier's beard and mustache, the emblem of the Knights around his neck, and wide gray eyes just now holding a glint of amusement.

"Greetings and honor, Master Wandor. I am Count Arlor."

"Honor and greetings, my lord. His Majesty's man of all work?"

"Your description, not mine, but it will serve. You've come at a good time. His Majesty has dealt with his lunch, and now would doubtless prefer to deal with you at once. So let us not keep him waiting." The Count pulled a leather thong, somewhere far away a bell tinkled three times, and a much closer (or much louder) voice bellowed, "Enter!"

King Nond's carved oak chair was wide enough for three ordinary men, but he filled it completely. The massive high-cheeked head with its thatch of gray hair was set directly on a chest like the trunk of a tree; at the end of long corded thick arms, long-fingered hands thrust out from the sleeves of a yellow chamber robe to lie clasped quietly on the ebony surface of the desk, between a silver inkpot and the ivory box that held the Royal Seal. Wandor went down on both knees and raised his hand in the Royal Salute; he would have done so to this man if he had met him in the lowest tavern in Trorim. The body was a gross monstrosity, but the manner and the gaze were beyond question that of a King.

"Rise, Master Wandor. You've proved you know court etiquette—but so do several thousand giggling fops and traitors. Do you know all the other things you're supposed to know?"

"Sire?"

"The Grand Master's report on you said"—the King fumbled under his robe and drew out a sheet of parchment —"'a magnificent young fighting animal at the height of his physical powers, expert in all the standard weapons, plus all those of the Knights, plus half a score more that few civilized men have ever heard of, with an admirably sure judgment and cool head beyond these.' How, my fine young fighting paragon, did you come to know how to use the weapons of the Knights?"

"The assistant arms-master of our House at Trorim was a landless knight. He was driven from his land by a baron whom he accused of kidnaping girls to sell to the stews of Benzor. The baron's family, incidentally, is now an ally of Duke Cragor.

"In any case, the knight took me in hand in the second year of my apprenticeship, when I was fourteen, and gave me an education in arms such as he might have given his own son and heir. It meant that I had little time to myself, but the results were well worth the trouble."

The King frowned. "Were they, Master? Do you think you could meet Count Arlor in single combat? He is reputed to be the finest hand in the kingdom with a dozen strange weapons."

"Under what conditions, sire?"

"To the death."

Wandor remembered his etiquette just in time enough to keep from gaping in open amazement. Half his mind was whirling in a frenzy, firmly convinced that at least one of the three people in the room was entirely and utterly mad; the other half was coolly analyzing the situation.

"With your permission, sire?"

"Certainly."

"Might I suggest Count Arlor have the choice of weapons?"

"That confident, eh? All right, my Lord Count—what do you choose?"

Count Arlor was silent for a moment, his eyes wandering over the trophies on the wall. Then a long arm shot out. "Those Costurn daggers. Do you know the proper Costurn fighting style, Master?" His voice was clipped and cold.

"Stripped to the waist and barefoot, with dagger in right hand and cloak wound around the left arm. Greater honor in killing with the edge than with the point."

"Well said." The Count began pulling off his tunic.

Five minutes later they were facing each other in the center of the room, stripped down to fighting garb, each watching the other intently, both conscious that King

Nond was leaning back in his chair, hands crossed over his stomach, watching *them*.

Wandor ran through the Short Form of the Duelist's Prayer, and added a brief prayer of his own that with King Nond apparently gone mad, the Five Gods should unite and watch over the Kingdom and guard it from Duke Cragor. Then he raised his dagger to eye-level in salute, thrust his cloak-wrapped left arm forward, and stepped out to do battle.

They felt each other out for the first two minutes, and Wandor discovered that Count Arlor's reputation was as well earned as his own. The man had great skill, plus a slight advantage in reach. Wandor judged that he himself was the stronger of the two, but that made little difference with the light, razor-sharp Costurn daggers. And if the duel was to be to the death, Arlor had as much reason as Wandor to give of his best.

But if it wasn't really to the death? Of course! Wandor's lips shaped a silent curse at his own stupidity. He had been showing the wits of a fresh-joined apprentice, not to have thought of this test before. Now he could move to carry it out. And if he was wrong—what chance had he of getting out of Manga Castle alive even if he did kill Arlor?

Wandor feinted once, then quickly shifted the direction of his thrust, pivoting on the balls of his feet the slight extra fraction of inch that would give the Count a clear opening at his throat. He saw the Count's blade lash out, flashing within an inch of his cheek. Wandor nearly laughed out loud. Good! Now to finish this farce and permit the King to proceed about his business.

Suddenly the Count found himself parrying slashes and thrusts that came blazing out of nowhere in a pattern that defied prediction. In desperation, he raked his edge along Wandor's dagger arm, and saw it open in a red slash from wrist to elbow. . . .

And seconds later he saw Wandor leap backward five feet in a single cat-footed bound, and with a motion too swift to follow flip the dagger from right hand to left. In the next seconds, any remaining hope in Arlor's mind vanished as the dagger came darting in with the same deadly precision. The only thing remaining to him now. . . .

Arlor's right hand darted up in an overhand thrust, but his left hand and arm suddenly whipped forward, fist clenched and stabbing at Wandor's groin. Wander pivoted on one foot, bending at the waist. The dagger thrust sailed over his shoulder and Arlor's arm crashed into his collarbone; the fist rode up on his hipbone; Arlor reeled forward, hopelessly off-balance—and found his right arm suddenly seized by Wandor's own "wounded" right arm with a savage downward thrust. Arlor crashed forward on his knees, and split-seconds later was spread-eagled on the stone floor, with Wandor's body weighing him down and Wandor's dagger a hair's breath from the back of his neck.

There was a roaring in the chamber. King Nond was laughing. Wandor stood up, turned toward the King, and bowed. "Have I your Majesty's consent to spare him? He fought well."

"He did indeed. But why should you wish to spare him?"

"First, because my honor as a Duelist demands that a brave man should not pay the supreme penalty for weaknesses beyond his fault. Second, because you never intended me to kill him at all."

"Oh?" Thick lips tightened inquiringly.

"I'll admit my first belief was that your Majesty had gone mad—I beg your pardon, sire. But it then occurred to me to test Count Arlor, by deliberately giving him an opening that no fighter fit to be out of the nursery would pass up. He did his best to make it look like a true error—but his best was not good enough. After that, I set myself to end the business as quickly as possible, although his slashing my arm slowed me up somewhat."

He swallowed. "Besides, unless you *had* gone mad, why would you risk the death of Count Arlor at the hands of an ordinary Master Duelist? He is your most reliable ally among the nobility, and you would find it hard to replace him."

"I must correct you, Master Wandor. I would find it *impossible* to replace him. How do you know all this?"

"People talk, your Majesty—Duke Cragor's ambitions are common knowledge, and those who hate him—most of your subjects, I'll wager—keep watch for any moves you make against him. Count Arlor's name is mentioned far too often for one to avoid noticing it."

"Provided that one keep's one's eyes and ears open, a thing few people seem to do these days. No matter, *you* do. Your wits are clearly as sharp and quick as your blades. Which is good, because you will need all that you have of both when you cross the ocean and reach the South Marches of the Viceroyalty of the East."

VI

Wandor was silent, although he had no idea what King Nond thought he could do in those half-tamed lands beyond the ocean. He nodded silently.

The King continued: "The leading noble of the March lands is Baron Oman Delvor. He is the leading noble there because I made him so, thirty years ago, for his services when I conquered the Viceroyalty." He was silent for a moment, and Wandor knew he must be thinking of the distant days when he had led a thousand ships and fifty thousand fighting men across the ocean, to bring the lands of the Khindi under the rule of the Kingdom of Benzos—the greatest conquest any of its Kings had made in over a century.

"I was a warrior, then," the King went on. "And there was nothing I would not have trusted to Baron Delvor—a poor knight he was then, but his integrity was stone-hard and his sword as sharp as Master Wandor's here. So I gave him his rightful share of the spoils, and left him to tame ten thousand square miles of forests and hills and plains and skulking bands of Khindi. He tamed them, settled them with hard-working peasants and just and loyal knights, and made them his home."

The King shook his head. "Now Duke Cragor has his eyes on the Viceroyalty, which he must have safe before he can strike safely at me here in Benzos. The Viceroy he has bought or coerced—I do not know how, for I thought the man loyal when I appointed him. The governor of the South Marches is one of Cragor's trusted henchmen—a low-born fellow, with nothing of rank or dignity or wit to claim the post, only a dog's loyalty to Cragor. The lesser nobles and knights have abandoned the struggle against Cragor, out of a fear or avarice, all but those few who shelter under the wings of House Delvor. Baron Delvor is the last refuge in the Viceroyalty for the loyal, and he needs help.

"He needs a man with nimble wits and an equally nimble sword blade, one who can act as his agent and watchdog and spy, one whom he can trust as I once trusted him. I am sending him one whom I hope will prove such a man—you, Master Wandor."

Both the praise and the honor were so great and so unexpected that Wandor was momentarily struck dumb. Then he said quietly, "I hope your Majesty's high confidence will not prove ill-placed."

King Nond waved the deprecating remark away with a fly-shooing gesture of both hands. "Save the modest manner for those you need to impress. To return to your mission: you will have the title of House Duelist—and *don't* start twittering about how your honor as a Master of the Order forbids you to take such a menial post. The title will be largely a disguise, although you may have to fight a few duels, since Baron Delvor has no sons and quite some few enemies who might try to curry favor with Cragor by seeing to eliminate him in a duel. But that will be at most the tenth part of what you do; the rest will depend on your wit and Baron Delvor's need and Duke Cragor's threats."

The King settled back in his chair—it creaked under his weight—and smiled thinly at Wandor. "Your greatest virtue, apart from everything else, is that Cragor will have no idea that you are really destined to be the mainstay of Baron Delvor. He is arrogant beyond belief; he thinks the Order of Duelists is a grubby band of cheap bravos, and he knows little and cares less about the reputations of its members. You will be one of the last persons he'd be capable of suspecting."

Wandor gulped. To speak out now might cost him the mission, and with it chances of glory, honor, adventure, and service to the King, but to remain silent would also tarnish his honor. He swallowed twice, clutched the arms of his chair, and spoke.

"Your Majesty?"

"Yes, Master Wandor?"

"I am afraid Duke Cragor does suspect me of being dangerous to him. You see. . . ." And he went on to tell of his adventures in the hills, omitting the episode beneath Mount Pendwyr as usual, while watching the King's face harden into something like the color and consistency of cold-worked bronze. By the time he had finished telling of the battle in the ghetto, the King's face had risen to an alarming shade of purple, while Count Arlor's eyes roamed about the room like those of a man seeking shelter from an approaching storm. Wandor finished his recital, there was a moment's silence, then——

"All the gods damn and curse and torment and burn Duke Cragor in the hottest fires of the uttermost depths of slimy filthy hell! May he see his limbs wither and rot! May black leprosy and foul rotting afflict him! May the gods visit on him and all of his——"

"Your Majesty!" gasped Count Arlor. "Spare your daughter!"

"My *daughter*. My gentle, kind, good, poetic, helpless little *curse* from the gods! If they had to deny me a son, why could they not show at least as much mercy as they did to Baron Delvor? They gave him a daughter fit to be a staff and a comfort, not a weight around his neck. Yes, Count Arlor, I know you love my poor pitiful submissive little Anya. And perhaps she loves you. So go—go and ask her, ask her to fly from Duke Cragor, from his insults and scorn and flaunting of mistresses and blows and foul temper. Will she follow you? Will she suddenly transform herself into Delvor's magnificent Gwynna? To be sure, she will—when Mount Pendwyr rises in fire and splits the hills open and scatters them to the sea!"

The King surged up from his chair. Wandor and Arlor dropped to their knees. He looked at them, then said tonelessly, "At least we know now that the Sthi are indeed hostile to Cragor. My Lord Count, make a note of that fact." He stalked out.

Wandor and the Count stood staring at each other for several minutes in silence. It was the Count who finally spoke.

"His Majesty has spoken. Now, Master Wandor, on the little matter of getting you across three thousand miles of ocean to the Viceroyalty . . . A merchant ship, the *Red Pearl* under a Captain Thargor who has executed royal commissions before and so knows what to do, will be dropping down the river from Benzor tomorrow morning. She will stop at the arsenal at the head of the Manga Canal to pick up a load of weapons and armor for the infantry regiments in the royal garrison of the Viceroyalty. She will also pick up you and your servant."

"Servant?"

"Yes. The King is sending one of his household Freedmen—a big Sea Folker, handy with an ax—along with you as servant, guard, and so on. Unless you claim to have eyes in the back of your head?"

"No."

"I didn't think so. I'll send for the man in a little while, and make arrangements for the two of you to be discreetly quartered somewhere in the keep tonight. Cragor's probably heard you're in town, so I doubt if there's an inn within thirty miles where you could sleep tonight with any great hope of waking up in the morning with your head still on your shoulders."

The Count stood up and pulled the bell cord. "And now, before we do anything else, I am going to have some food sent up. I was so busy keeping various people with allegedly urgent business from disturbing his Majesty's lunch that I never got to eat my own. And by the time he comes down from his walk on the roof, he will have it firmly fixed in his head that Duke Cragor's discovering your identity—never mind how—demands that I *immediately* saddle up and ride five hundred miles up hill and down dale to Trorim to personally investigate possible spies in the Governor's household, the garrison, and probably your own Order as well. And *that* means this meal will be my last civilized one for at least ten days. I hope you're hungry."

Wandor began the meal hungry, but by the time he had waded through roast veal, mutton pasty, raisin-stuffed capon, herb bread, early melon, and his fair share of a bowl of wine, he was so no longer. As they relaxed over the last of that wine, a thought suddenly entered Wandor's mind; he immediately put it into words.

"Baron Delvor has a daughter, does he? Is there anything I should know beforehand about her? I mean is she likely to help or hinder my efforts?"

Count Arlor put his cup down and considered the question for a moment, then replied: "Help, I think. But only after her own fashion. She's as wild and untamable as a young falcon—and far more beautiful. The most unbelievable red hair, white skin, slim and graceful and quick as a young gazelle. Rides and pulls a bow with the best, and, as for swordsmanship, we had a practice round the last time I saw her. She must have been, oh, fourteen or so. And I had to extend myself to the fullest to beat her."

Wandor looked at the Count, looked at his long frame and long limbs, remembered his demonstrated skill with weapons, tried to imagine a fourteen-year-old girl capable of matching him. Tried and failed. "Is that all about—Gwynna, I think that was her name?"

Arlor shook his head slowly. "I wish that were all. But there are rumors of more. Rumors that she has powers."

Wandor smiled. "All beautiful women have at least one power—that of enslaving and devastating men with their beauty. We Duelists are trained to remain immune to that power, at least until we lay down our swords. So——"

"So stop letting your tongue run ahead of your wits," snapped Arlor. "I mean the Power—Ancient Days magic, spell-working and animal speech and no one knows what else."

He shook his head. "It is *perhaps* just rumor. But I do know this—her servants were obviously in mortal fear of her, and I *saw* a pair of eagles fly down and sit on her windowsill for an hour while she crooned to them in a voice that made my flesh crawl on my bones. It is said one nursemaid who tried to beat her disappeared without a trace, this when she was eleven.

"And above everything, when she was fourteen, in fact just after I last saw her, she went alone across the Silver Mountains out to the Plains, and there the Red Seers of the Plainsmen initiated her into their rites and skills. And what those hold of the ancient magic, for good and evil both, the demons below only know." He shuddered. "Don't play any games with her, Master Wandor, or you may discover the true extent of her power to your cost." He pulled the bell cord again. "Time for you to meet your servant."

The servant swept in through the door, stooping slightly, then straightened to his full height and stood silently. He was half a head taller than even Count Arlor, and would have made two of him in width. Wandor looked him up and down, noticed the short-handled single-hand ax stuck in his wide metal-link belt, the enormous muscles bulging under the rough woolen robe, and nodded to himself in satisfaction.

"What is your name, Sea Folker?"

"I am called Berek, Master. I have thirty years. I was taken in the twentieth of them and freed by King Nond to become of his Household in the twenty-fifth of them."

"Good. And what are your weapons?"

"This ax, Greenfoam, which I carry. And my great ax, Thunderstone."

Wandor nodded again. The normal Sea Folker great ax was five feet long, with an ironwood handle and a double-edged head weighing ten pounds or more. If this out-sized Sea Folker Berek carried an ax as out-sized as himself, it would be a good weapon to have on one's side. He turned to Count Arlor.

"My Lord, would you please get us a clean cup—a small one will do."

Arlor shrugged and went over to a cupboard, returning with a small silver cup. Wandor took it from him and handed it to Berek, then picked up one of the Costurn daggers from the table, held it between his hands for about a minute while his lips moved silently in prayer, then handed it also to Berek.

The huge man took up the daggar in his right hand, placed the cup on the table, and with the dagger drew a long shallow slash down his left arm. Then he held the arm over the goblet until about two fingers' depth of blood had flowed into it, picked up the goblet, and handed it back to Wandor, saying, "This my blood to my master and lord, from this day forth, by my honor."

"This his blood from my faithful Berek, who shall have from me that which I have from him, from this day forth, by my honor." Wandor raised the cup and emptied it at one swallow. Out of the corner of one eye, he noticed the Count turning slightly green in the face, so he said hastily, "My thanks, Berek. Now—you will find my gear at the foot of the keep staircase. Go and ask the steward where to take it, and show them this," and he pulled off his Master's emblem and handed it to Berek. The giant bowed deeply and backed out of the room.

Wandor turned to Count Arlor and grinned. "You are wondering what that was all about, aren't you?"

The Count nodded. Wandor said, "The Oath of the Drunk Blood is the ultimate oath of fealty among the Sea Folk. The blood he gave me to drink is the symbol of the blood he will shed without fear or stint in my service. A man who forswears that oath is cast out of his clan and

46

tribe as an outlaw, and they believe that when he dies (which is usually soon), he suffers torments for which there are no words in any language, including that of the Sea Folk."

Count Arlor nodded and looked at the hourglass. "His Majesty will be down from the roof again within a few minutes. I think you had best be about equipping yourself for the journey. The seneschal and his stewards have orders to give you free run of the storerooms for anything you might need, from armor to love potions."

He stood up and thrust out his hand. "If the King has business for me, and he usually does, I much doubt that I will see you again before you leave. So"—and they joined right hands and raised the left ones in the palm-outward salute of honor and farewell—"may the gods have you in their keeping, that you may live to strike good blows for the King and afterward to receive your due honor for your services."

"May the gods deal likewise with you," said Wandor, and strode out.

VII

WANDOR LEANED over the quarterdeck rail of the *Red Pearl* and watched the lighthouse on Blackstone Point north of Tafardos drop astern. Ahead, so Captain Thargor had told him, lay five or more weeks of sailing, until they raised the coast of the Viceroyalty, five weeks at the mercy of waves and wind and the Sea Folk raiding squadrons.

Footsteps thumped behind him; he turned and stared into the weather-worn red face of Captain Thargor. "Afternoon, Captain."

"Afternoon, Master Wandor. Did you sleep well last night—your first ever at sea if you tell me truly?"

"True, Captain. I did sleep well, but I expected to; if I'm any judge, you've a good ship here."

"If you've never spent a night at sea, you're no judge. But *Pearl's* a good ship just the same, and a good stout crew—we'd not have a royal charter nor a royal cargo were it otherwise. With luck, we'll fetch Yost without troubling the Sea Spirits with our howling for help. But the Sea Folk are something else, they're becoming as much a menace as wind and sea, which is no fit thing for an old seaman like myself to say, but true."

He paused to spit over the lee rail. "Worse beyond that, they've taken to going after the royal-charter ships above all else; they'll let slip three or four fat prizes of ordinary merchantmen to capture a skiff with the royal banner. They live by their prizes, so there must be somebody making it worth their while to do this, let me tell you."

Wandor frowned. "Perhaps Duke Cragor?"

"I name no names without proof, but who else could it be?"

Wandor nodded. "True. But couldn't you perhaps haul down that royal banner, and look like an ordinary ship?"

Thargor grunted. "No good would that do, for *Pearl*'s been a royal-charter since I took command ten years ago. And that's known all across the ocean by now. And besides: would you take off your Duelist's badge to save having to fight a duel?"

Wandor shook his head; Thargor grunted again. "No more would I take down that banner. I'll rely on the gods and the sea spirits and the winds and the good right arms of my men down there to save me from the Sea Folk. And you and that Berek of yours may prove some help on this voyage."

The two men looked forward, past the break of the quarterdeck and the deckhouse with its stacked boats, to where Berek stood by the mainmast with Thunderstone in his hands and Greenfoam slung at his belt. About half a cord of firewood was piled by the hatch with a ship's boy squatting beside it. The boy placed a log on the deck and darted aside; Thunderstone flashed skyward and came down with a crash. The log flew into two pieces which leaped high in the air and clattered back again on to the deck.

Thargor frowned. "If that barbarian puts his ax through my deck, His Majesty'll be getting a bill for repairs."

"Don't worry, Captain. You've seen Sea Folker axes in action—you know they can swing at an egg and crack it without breaking."

"I've indeed seen far too many of them in action, Master Wandor. And I'm hoping to see none this voyage."

Captain Thargor's hope was in vain. One windless dawn three weeks later, off the coast of Yand Island, the growing light revealed two pairs of elongated lateen sails rising over the horizon. Captain Thargor, roused by the look-out, scrambled up the rigging to the crow's nest and looked out at them. "Sea Folk," he said quietly, and called down the news to the deck.

Instantly, the heavy bronze alarm gong on the foremast was sounded, and the ship came alive with men rushing about to dump the galley fire, clear away furniture, and snatch their weapons and armor out of the arms' chests. Wandor and Berek came on deck, Wandor full-armed down to his boot knives, Berek naked except for breech cloth and the broad belt from which Greenfoam dangled, while Thunderstone swung in his gigantic hands.

Wandor leaned his bow and quiver against the railing and approached Captain Thargor. "How soon will they be up with us, Captain?"

"We're not going anywhere fast, not with this calm, so my wager is they'll come up slow and easy, to spare their strength. You know their fighters and their oarsmen are the same, I suppose?"

"I do. How many will they have?"

"Above fifty in each ship. We have barely forty who can swing a blade. And they're carring their black sails, which means they're not long out from port and will be taking no prisoners." He sighed. "We may give them both a good hiding before they take us, but I won't hope for much more."

Wandor frowned and looked aft. "Captain, do you suppose you could break out some of the cargo? It's mostly arms and armor, and I have a few ideas for using them that might give us a better chance."

"Break into his Majesty's cargo? The Viceroy'd have me head for it!"

"Better the Viceroy than the Sea Folk, Captain."

Thargor shrugged and turned away to begin bellowing orders. Wandor unbuckled his belt, took a prybar, and began to work on the crates as they were hauled up from below, while on the horizon the two grim shapes moved closer . . . closer . . . closer. . . .

When the two Sea Folk ships came sliding up alongside the *Red Pearl* half an hour later, they saw a typical undermanned and overloaded merchantman, her sails set in a lubberly fashion with the rigging hanging in festoons, her decks littered with lumber and rolled-up sails and bare of crew except for the look-out staring myopically from the crow's nest and two half-naked ruffians at the helm. One on each side, the raiders backed their oars and drifted in toward their prey, while the crews began laying down the oars and pulling their longswords and axes out from beneath the rowing benches.

Crash! The *Pearl*'s topsail yard jerked up in its slings as the festooned rigging suddenly tightened, tipped up, and came lancing down on to and through the deck of the nearer enemy ship, spearing her like a salmon.

Twang! Whizz! Thump! Five times in rapid succession, as four men rose up beside the lookout and all five aimed their crossbows and fired. The helmsman of the other raider clutched his throat and crumpled; beside him fell his captain, toppling against the helm and driving it hard over so that the ship swung and crunched up hard against the *Pearl*'s side.

Grapnels arched through the air to claw the rigging and railings of both enemy ships, as the rolled-up sails on the *Pearl*'s deck suddenly unrolled and disgorged armed men. The crew of one enemy ship drew their swords and started hacking at the grapnel lines, and abruptly two of them sprouted arrows in their chests as Wandor's bow twanged.

Then there was a mighty crashing of wood and clanging of metal as the hatch covers flew across the decks and the rest of the *Red Pearl*'s crew swarmed out of the hold and over the bulwarks on to the enemy's deck. The royal army's still-oiled armor protected their bodies, royal swords swung in their hands, shields bearing the royal crest blocked enemy blows and drove into enemy faces, as they leaped down on to the stunned Sea Folk.

Wandor dropped two more men with his bow, then the tangle on the enemy decks became so complete that it was no longer safe to shoot into the press. He drew his sword and led Berek forward to meet Captain Thargor, who was waving his arms about and frantically screaming words that gradually took shape as "The other ship! The other ship!"

Wandor spun around to look. All but two or three of the *Pearl*'s crew had leaped down on the enemy ship to port, the one speared by the topsail yard. Her decks were a seething cauldron of struggling men and flashing weapons. To starboard, the few hardy boarders were being cut down, and even as Wandor watched, the stern grapnel line parted and the enemy ship began to swing clear, her crew leaning furiously to their oars.

"Stop them!" screamed Thargor. "They'll get away and bring the whole squadron to hunt us down and we'll all die by slow torture! Stop them!"

Wandor's throwing knife flashed across the widening space of sea into the helmsman's arm, and as he screamed and reeled clear of the helm, Wandor swung his feet over the bulwarks, braced himself against the catheads, and leaped wildly outwards. He twisted in midair as a pike thrust darted within an inch of his chest, then landed almost on top of a smallish man who was clawing a long dagger out of his belt.

Planks thundered beside Wander as Berek leaped down, and air parted with a swish as Thunderstone arched into the press of men to smash two of them dead on the deck. Wandor brought his knee up sharply, and the daggerman gasped and reeled back just far enough for Wandor's own dagger to leap free and into his chest. Then Wandor sprang clear, fetching up against the bulwarks, as Berek hacked down another man and stepped up beside him.

A moment's pause. Wandor looked around, saw the Sea Folk drawing back to gather their strength, saw the *Red Pearl*'s side receding, saw the enemy begin to point at Berek, heard a cry of horror from one of them. *"It is Berek Strong-Ax!"* Suddenly he had to force himself not to turn his eyes away from the enemy and stare at Berek.

Berek was nudging him. "Forward, Master, forward we must go." Wandor nodded. He drew himself back hard against the bulwarks, flexed his knees, and he and Berek leaped forward together.

Dagger into one man's face, sword blade across another's throat, fist into another's groin, Thunderstone rising and falling with crashes and screams and thuds in its wake, a blade raking across his own ribs and the blood flowing free and hot. Then they were at the bow, and Wandor dropped to the deck and rolled as an arrow flashed by him and quivered in the bulkhead.

His head was against a massive barrel, his feet against a bronze box. Berek reached across his master's body, dragged him to his feet, and swung Thunderstone at the barrel. Oil gushed out, brown and shining. He snatched up the bronze box, ripped off the catch with one hand, upended it with the other. Hot coals arched out, fell, ignited the oil on the deck. A river of fire flowed across the deck of the ship, cutting Wandor and Berek off from the crew.

Wandor looked past the shimmering flames and saw a man running forward with a bow. Berek caught at his arm. "There are more barrels below, Master. We must be for the sea," and gestured over the side. Wandor nodded, thrust his sword into its scabbard, and hurled himself low over the bulwarks into the sea.

As Berek splashed into the water behind him, Wandor turned to watch the burning ship. The whole deck forward was ablaze, and fire was running up the tarred rigging and igniting the tight-rolled sails on their yards. Tongues of fire began to flicker out of gaping seams as tinder-dry planking caught the flames. As he watched, he saw armor beginning to clang to the deck and naked figures hurling themselves over the side. He turned his back on the scene and began to swim, cutting strongly through the water until his reaching arms struck something hard.

He looked up. The *Red Pearl*'s weed-grown side loomed above them, and two ropes came snaking down from the deck. As they reached the deck, the barrels below in the burning Sea Folk ship caught fire, and a monstrous gushing mass of flame erupted through the planking to engulf her from bow to stern, as the last of her people leaped over the side.

On the other side of the *Red Pearl*, the impaled enemy ship was lying far over to port, oars floating about her, air bubbling slowly and inexorably out of her as she rocked lower and lower in the slight swell. The *Pearl*'s crew swarmed around Wandor, showing him their hacked armor and bloodied swords, pounding him on the back, and shouting praise until Thargor pushed through them and stepped up to Wandor.

"Well done, Master Wandor. Both ships are finished, and sharks'll have the swimmers before nightfall. Now, I think——"

But Wandor was ignoring the Captain. Instead he turned to Berek and said quietly, "Your battle name is truly Strong-Ax?"

"Yes. I left it among my people when I was captured, not long after I became a full warrior. Does it displease my Master?"

Wandor's lips said no, but his mind was elsewhere. The gold-lit firepit beneath Mount Pendwyr, which had receded to the dim level of a dream, came back to him full force. "Go and win the faith of Strong-Ax," the Guardian had said. He had done so. How many more specters out of the Testing of the Five-Crowned King would rise to haunt him, here out in the bright living world where such things should not be? The first one had come to him amid a battle out at sea; where would the next one come?

The gods, it is said, make a path for those who make a path for themselves. And so it seemed for the *Red Pearl*. That night the wind rose, fresh and clean and brisk, and blew and kept on blowing for two weeks, until a bright dawn when Wandor stood on the *Pearl*'s focs'le with Berek and watched the blue-black towers of Yost and the pine-clad hills behind it climb out of the whitecapped sea.

He turned to Berek. "Is everything packed tightly? Did you polish my sword?"

Berek looked hurt. "Master, I am not a child. I have

done what is needful for our weapons. And may I ask you —how is your wound?"

Wandor ran an experimental hand around his ribs. "Sore, but healing well enough. It will not slow me down enough to matter."

"Good!"

They stood in silence until Thargor came up to them, and Berek discreetly withdrew. Then the Captain went through the hand-clasp and salute of honor with Wandor, and said: "Gods be with you, Master. You saved my ship. I only wish I could do as much for you there"— he gestured toward the approaching shore— "as you've done for me out here."

Wandor grinned. "Get me into Yost before noon, and I'll be riding up-country by nightfall. If Duke Cragor wants to pursue me out into the Marches, it may cost him more than I'm worth. And as for enemies other than Duke Cragor—the enemies of the spirit world—you and I and all creatures of flesh and blood are equally helpless against them." Even, he added silently, when they seem to be on one's own side

VIII

ABOUT THE TIME the rising west wind was carrying the *Red Pearl* away from Yand Island and the floating debris of her victims, a small ship flying a black-and-red banner slipped into the harbor of Fors, capital city of the Viceroyalty of the east. Her anchor went down, her crew bustled about on deck, and soon a boat put off for shore, rowed by six men.

Two others sat in the stern of the boat. One was tall and skull-faced, with a spade-shaped black beard and close-cropped black hair under a broad-brimmed red-velvet hat. Under his red-silk tunic was a black chain-mail shirt; on his feet were heavy riding boots with gleaming spurs.

The other was short and pale and round-faced, dressed wholly in a purple so dark as to be almost black from his square cap to his plain leather sandals. On his lap was a long black stick with a gold tip, and his feet rested on a large ebony-faced box with silvered hinges and a triangular badge.

The boat bumped against the quay; four armed men ran down to help the two men in the boat mount the stairs, four more advanced holding horses. The two from the boat mounted, their eight guards mounted after them, and the whole party went clattering up the streets of Fors toward the Viceregal Palace.

As they passed, heads popped out of doors and windows —and abruptly popped back in. When people saw the skull-faced man, they muttered, "There's the Black Duke again," or "Wonder what's Duke Cragor doin' over here again," or perhaps, "Not the Duke *again*! I hope he didn't bring his Household. They drank the town dry and ate it bare the last time he came." But when they saw the short pale figure riding behind Cragor, they gasped, "Kaldmor the Dark!" and ran as fast as they could into the rooms farthest from the streets, shutting doors and windows and taking their children and praying to all the gods and spirits they could think of.

The meeting of Duke Cragor and his supporters was held in a room high in the south tower of the Viceregal Palace, with a window looking out toward those south Marches where Baron Delvor stood against the Duke. The Viceroy was not present. He never was. Duke Cragor's habit was to settle matters involving the Viceroyalty without regard to the land's nominal overlord, even though the man was supposed to be one of his loyal supporters. However, Duke Cragor did not regard him as such—and the Black Duke's opinion was the only one that counted in such matters.

There *were* at the meeting Baron Galkor, Governor of the south Marches, and Sir Festan Jalgath, Marshall of the Viceroyalty and commander of the royal garrison there. They rose as the Duke and Kalmor entered, bowed deeply, and settled themselves again to wait for the Duke to speak.

When he did, he was brief and pointed, as always. "Our final blow to purge the Kingdom of His Majesty's enemies is barely a year away, yet we dare not act without securing beyond question a firm base here in the Viceroyalty. In this we have failed." He would have gladly spoken even more bluntly, but with Sir Festan—the obstinately loyal Sir Festan—present, he could not.

"Baron Delvor's strength in the south March is as great as ever. All the lords and gentry look to him for leadership; all the peasants and merchants look to him for justice. Some knights are kept from joining him only by all the bribery and fear we can muster. The coastal fiefs and the north March follow us but close to the sea they do so partly from fear of the Sea Folk."

He slapped his hand down on the table with a whip-cracking noise. "And *now* we hear the King is sending an agent, a chosen agent, to House Delvor to aid it in its struggle to keep the Viceroyalty for the King. That was what finally decided me to take ship—and *such* a ship—to see for myself what a shambles you men have made of our affairs here."

Baron Galkor smiled. "My Lord, the King has sent *one* agent? Only one? Why then the sudden haste?"

"There would be no haste, Galkor, if the agent were

56

such as you are given to hiring—a back-alley brawler who would kill for a full meal and enough wine to get drunk on. But King Nond is no fool, and neither will be his agent."

The Duke rang for wine, and while it was being brought he went on. "This agent passes as a House Master of the Order of Duelists. No doubt he is in fact one of Nond's trusted house knights; the Order of Duelists could hardly be expected to produce such a fighting man as he appears to be. A band of my men pursued him into the forests near Mount Pendwyr—and they never came out. But this agent himself survived whatever befell them, broke up a pogrom among the Khindi outside Benzor, and then vanished. If he crosses the ocean safe from the Sea Folk, he will probably make for Yost and it is there we must watch for him. Where *you* must watch for him Galkor."

"Indeed," said Galkor angrily. If your men perished near Pendwyr the accursed—what if this agent has the power? What am I to do against a man who may be able to conjure up aid from the spirit world at need?"

"That is Kaldmor's concern, Galkor, and for that I have asked him to come with me. Neither the Knights nor the Duelists permit a man with the power among them. All the man's talents—and be warned, they will be great—will be natural. But he must be caught and dealt with before he escapes to the shelter of House Delvor."

"Surely, your companion," Galkor said, with a nervous look at Kaldmor, "can use his—arts—against this man if need be, no matter where he is?"

"No sorcerer, not even I, can strike at a man beneath the aura of the Lady Gwynna of Delvor," said Kaldmor. He seemed to regard this as a sufficient and final explanation. Both Galkor and Sir Feston looked openly skeptical. The sorcerer glared at them, and said very slowly, as though explaining the matter to a child, *"No* sorcerer, I said. Standing against me alone and unaided, the lady would indeed be bested. But she will never do that, being no fool. Rather, she will call upon all the Red Seers of the Plainsmen. They will call upon all their powers. To best the Lady Gwynna would thus mean not a single combat, but besting every Red Seer from the Silver Mountains to Worldrim beyond the Plains. Call me to your aid before this agent is within the March lands or I can do nothing safely against him."

"You alone lack the power to best the Lady Gwynna—

perhaps," said Galkor. "But what of rumors we heard, that *you* yourself serve strange masters, and can call *them* to your aid. What——"

"What is babbled by fools and madmen is no concern of mine!" snapped Kaldmor. "This I tell you as the truth which you would do well not to doubt. *I call no one* to my aid. I am Kaldmor the Dark. I am that by which all other sorcerers are judged and measured. And I am not merciful toward wine-swollen fools with loose tongues and wit-poor spirits."

Galkor was silent, and this seemed to content Kaldmor, much to the relief of Sir Festan, who found all this talk of conjuring up demons and spirits rather ungentlemanly, particularly when applied to a good warrior and an honorable worshiper of the Five Gods such as Baron Delvor. He decided to return the discussion to its proper course.

"My lords, it seems that no sorcery can readily be used against this agent, unless we have the good fortune to identify him before he reaches the Marches. What then are we to do?" He ignored Kaldmor's muttered curses.

"Do?" said Cragor. "The same as before, only with none of the blundering there has been until now. Watch for any chance to force Delvor into a provocative or disloyal move. Strengthen our own forces, win over the gentry, drill our own troops, and silence the disloyal by whatever means may be needed. And for the moment, call on all our natural powers to deal with this agent."

IX

THE AIR HUNG still and thick around Castle Delvor, heavy and sticky with the coming rain. Baron Oman Delvor shifted uncomfortably in the great chair and listened to the familiar succession of sounds that marked his daughter's homecoming from the hunt.

First came the clatter of her mare's hooves on the stone of the castle courtyard. Then came the running feet of the servants and the groom, darting out to relieve her of whatever she had brought back and take the mare to the stables. There was the snarl of the two great hunting leopards as some inexperienced stablehand moved too close. Gwynna's own voice, low and gentle and bell-clear, calmed the great cats. And then, mounting the stairs of the Great Hall, the sound of riding boots and jingling spurs and the pad-pad-pad of the leopards drew near. Baron Delvor rose and went to meet his daughter.

She came up the stairs with the same flowing grace as the leopards running beside her. For perhaps the hundredth time, her father thought how much like them she was—quick and slender and graceful, a beautiful and deadly young animal. She strode up to him and swept the broad-brimmed green-leather hat with its golden feather off her head. Her flame-hued hair seemed to light up the dim hall, and the Baron remembered the whispers he had heard among the servant girls of how Gwynna's hair sometimes glowed in the dark with a light of its own.

She held out both hands to him; he took them and said: "Greetings, daughter. How was the hunting?"

"Only fair. Avla brought down a young buck antelope out beyond Hartshorne Hill, but the animals seem to have

59

gone to earth. I knew there was a great storm coming, so I came home before it broke."

As always, the Baron suppressed a cold, questing thought: how did she *know* there was a storm coming? Her mother—gentle Harla, in her grave in the pine-furred hills these fifteen years—had understood Gwynna; she might have known the answer to that question. He never would. To him there was left nothing but to watch Gwynna, and listen—and now and then tremble.

He put the thought aside and smiled approvingly. "Wise of you. No point in trying to prove once again that you're hardier than any of my huntsmen—I and they both know it; we've known it since you were seventeen and were out four days in that blizzard."

Gwynna laughed. "You'll never believe I honestly lost my way, will you, Father?"

He shook his head. "You're too good a woodsman for me to believe that, Gwynna." He patted her shoulder. "Go and prepare yourself for dinner. You know how Sir Gar is."

She grimaced. "I do, indeed. Why does he run this backwoods stone warren as though it were a royal palace, and insist that I dress like a queen?"

"Because you can so easily look like one, my dear, and Sir Gar, old as he is, is still not too old to take pleasure in contemplating a beautiful woman."

The rain had come, riding in on the wind that howled around the castle, making the windows rattle and bang in their frames and the candles along the high table flicker and dance. Their light reflected old silver and gold and crystal and amber wine and Gwynna's hair, flowing down her shoulders from under a gold circlet.

Baron Delvor loosened his belt a notch and sighed gently. House Delvor had many things for which to thank Sir Gar Stendor, not least that he kept the service and the cooking impeccable—more suited to a royal palace than to this great austere stone pile, set here among the wind-thundering forests and hills of rippling grass.

He looked down the table to where his daughter sat. She was another thing in the castle more than worthy of a royal palace. Not that there was any great chance of her ever gracing one. What prince or king would find his way to Castle Delvor? And what would he say to finding his intended bride a wild young huntress able to ride and shoot and hawk and cross a blade with him or the best of his household?

If he said what the Baron suspected he would say, that would be an end of it, for Gwynna would never go to any man who would seek to tame her or break her like a wild animal—not of her own consent. And for the sake of Gwynna herself, the memory of her mother, the honor of House Delvor, and his own conscience before the Five Gods, the Baron had sworn solemnly never to force her into any match without her consent. Which would be a losing and hopeless cause, in any case. One slight move in that direction by him, and she would be gone like the birds in autumn, across river and forest and plain and mountain, to make her own life where and how the gods willed it.

Perhaps she would find something in this Duelist the King was sending as his agent—and then the Baron grinned ruefully to himself. He had allowed himself similar hopes of every presentable male coming to Castle Delvor these last four years, and what chance was there of the Duelist being presentable in any case? If he was prominent enough in his Order to attract the attention and earn the trust of King Nond, chances were he was a grizzled old warhorse, however shrewd and skilled he might be.

Young or old, ugly or handsome, the agent could be no more than a few days away. He might be landing at Yost even now. So now it was time for him to sit down with Sir Gar and Gwynna to plan how to make use of whatever talents the agent might be bringing to them.

He looked across the table to Sir Gar, standing in grim dignity by the kitchen door, and nodded. The old knight clapped his hands, and the servants streamed out of the kitchen and began to clear the table. The Baron stood up, and Gwynna followed him. "Sir Gar," he said, "when you have finished in here, meet us in the trophy room, with some fruit spirits if there are any." He wrapped his cloak around him, took Gwynna's arm, and strode out.

Sir Gar stepped through the door of the trophy room, followed by a servant with the decanter and glasses on a silver tray, and made his way across the room, over the pelt-strewn floor dappled with the distorted wavering shadows of the rows of hunting trophies on the wall, to where Gwynna and her father sat by the window. Gwynna had thrown a blue cloak over her gown. Both rose as Sir Gar approached. He handed the glasses from the tray and looked at the Baron.

"The King, may the gods preserve him," said the Baron, and drank.

"The King," echoed the other two, and emptied their glasses.

"Now," said Gwynna briskly, seeing the two men seemingly ready to settle down for a long convivial evening of old comrades' talk, "what more of this agent the King is sending to us?"

Her father shrugged. "You have read his letter; you know all that I do. 'A House Master of the Order of Duelists, in whom I am given by the Grand Master much reason to repose my confidence, the more in that he is not as yet known by Duke Cragor to be in my service.' The King gave no other details; it would seem that the man himself had not yet arrived at Benzor when the King sent off the letter."

Sir Gar bit back an oath. "Then for all we—or His Majesty—know this Duelist might be some base-born back-alley b-b-brawler. . . ." He became entangled in a flurry of "b's" for a moment, then went on. "A brawler, I say, little better than a hired daggerman. What good to us from such, I ask you?"

Baron Delvor smiled. "For one thing, he can be an extra guard. Need I remind you that we are two old men and a young woman, that we are all that stands between Duke Cragor and rule over the Viceroyalty, and that only the loyalty of our servants and our great distance from towns has kept knives out of our backs and poison out of our wine this long? Besides, if this man is indeed a House Master, he will be deadly with at least a dozen weapons, and no ordinary knifeman will have any chance of getting through him to us. No, the only fault I am prepared to find with this agent now is that he is one and not fifty or a hundred."

Gwynna sighed wearily. "Why do you people sit around moaning about his being 'one and not fifty or a hundred'? I have said before, let me ride across the Silver Mountains to the Plainsmen, speak to Zakonta—and I will return with a thousand times fifty men and women with bows and lances and swords to make Castle Delvor as safe as Manga Castle itself. And if we ever decide to strike at Duke Cragor first, instead of sitting and waiting for him to strike at us, then the Plainsmen would come to our aid in numbers like the sands of the sea beaches and——"

"Gwynna!" roared the Baron. "I have forbidden you to speak of alliances with those—those barbarians! One word of our bringing them across the mountains, and Duke Cragor would strike in a moment and all our allies would drop away like dead leaves and leave us naked to face the Black Duke! And what help would those fiends on horseback be then? *What, I ask you?*"

"Oh!" exclaimed Gwynna. "They're not fiends, they're not barbarians, they're—oh, what's the use of talking to a stone wall? All the gods deliver us from the wisdom of old men!" She jumped to her feet and stamped out of the room.

As the oak door boomed shut behind her, the Baron noticed Sir Gar making the formal sign of propitiation to the Five Gods. "She frightens you, Sir Gar?"

"Great gods above, yes! You never know what she'll propose next."

"She frightens me, too. There's not much of me in that girl. Most of it's her mother, and the rest is—well, something, and may the gods keep me ignorant of what it is for the years that remain to me!"

The seneschal nodded. "Still, if all else failed, and the Duke were already moving against us . . . she did go across the mountains when she was fourteen, remember that. What I fear is, suppose she went and failed? We'd never see her again in this world."

The Baron shook his head. "There's a chance of that, to be sure. But I would be more afraid of what might be unleashed if she went and succeeded."

X

YOST WAS THE smaller of the two cities of the Viceroyalty —smaller in population, smaller in all the amenities of civilized life, smaller in the area it controlled. Beyond a single day's good ride from its walls, the ploughed fields and neat cottages and broad roads leading from village to town gave way to rutted mud tracks, and then to meandering paths through the endless miles of forest, where only the single High Road offered a swift passage across the Marches to South Pass. The forest stretched on, green and silent, to the Silver Mountains, broken here and there by the rude castles and still-ruder huts of Marcher lords' estates, and filled with the outlaw bands and Khindi that normally made the outside world more than willing to leave the Marches be.

But within Yost, the hand of the Viceroy (meaning the hand of Duke Cragor, now) fell heavily, and Wandor knew the sooner he passed beyond the reach of that hand the better for him and his mission. Captain Thargor loaned them the services of two of his crew to carry their extra gear and two more to row them ashore, consigned them to the care of the gods, and turned back to unloading his cargo of now slightly used weapons and armor.

Wandor and Berek had their fair share of curious glances as they marched up the street from the quays. Though Wandor had his Master's emblem concealed beneath the jacket of his leather riding suit, the sword and daggers worn openly proclaimed him a fighting man, here as in Benzor. And Berek would have stood out in (and above) any crowd anywhere, even in his native lands to the north. Wandor was aware of the attention they were attracting, and guided their steps as fast as possible without attracting still more notice toward the Street of Stables.

They walked down the Street, amid the sound of whinnying and ringing hooves and the clang of smith's hammers and the smells of hay and horse-dung, looking at the signs jutting out into the street. The small livery stables would have few good horses; the large ones might have many—but also many eyes and ears ready and open to gather in sights and sounds for Duke Cragor. They finally compromised on a moderate-sized one, whose sign proclaimed it to be the home of "Jel Dogustam's Finest Steeds." ("I should hate to see his worst," muttered Wandor as they went in.)

Dogustam turned out be a youngish man of half-Hond, half-Khindi descent—the height and coloring of the former, the hooked nose and short dark hair of the latter—and aggressively eager to please. "And what would you noble sires be requiring today from my poor household?"

Wandor sighed. "Two good horses, with strength rather than speed, and fewer compliments if you please. We've a long journey ahead of us."

"Two good strong horses, yes, noble sirs. And if you would care to step out to the stable, we have the best in Yost for you to choose from." Wandor nodded to Berek and followed Dogustam out, keeping one hand within easy reach of his sword hilt.

"The best in Yost" actually turned out to be fairly presentable. After a few minutes' inspection, Wandor chose out a heavily built gray gelding for Berek and a smaller roan stallion for himself, and after a few minutes more bargaining paid out only a little more than he had intended to pay, and not really much more than the horses were worth. Too much bargaining would have been just another way of attracting attention to himself.

Dogustam swept the stack of silver florins into his strongbox, shoved it under the counter, and told two of his stablemen to have the horses saddled and bridled. "And where might two such noble—and warlike—gentlemen as you be going with these horses? If it's for fighting that you want them, perhaps you ought to reconsider your choices. I——"

"We're going north, if it's any concern of yours," said Wandor. "A brother of my companion—Sir Brechal—has promised us good service in guarding his lands against the Khindi. And he'll give us warsteeds if they prove needed."

"Ah, yes," said Dogustam. "Always fighting up there, always those wretches of Khindi without sense to come out and accept our noble Viceroy's offers of peace. Would you believe that they even make the Forest High Road so dangerous, no party of less than a hundred can get through it alive?"

"I've heard as much," said Wandor. "And now, we will wish you good day and the favor of the gods."

Once they were mounted and riding toward the city gates, Wandor turned to Berek and said, "I would have rather wished him long and loving torment at the hands of a legion of fiends. He said 'noble Viceroy' rather than 'noble King'—I would judge him in Cragor's pay, or perhaps even loyal to the Duke of his own free will."

They were almost at the East Gate when out of a side street marched a squad of soldiers, flanking a long shuffling line of chained prisoners. The soldiers were regular royal infantry—nothing noteworthy about them, except that they were all in full battle array, with a short throwing spear instead of the fourteen-foot long pike. It was the prisoners that caught Wandor's eye.

They were small to medium in height, well formed, stocky (as far as one could tell through the starvation and fatigue of slavery), with creamy brown-gold skins now caked with dirt and glossy black hair. Plainsmen! Wandor had read descriptions of them, and had even seen a few of them as carefully guarded house slaves in a few of the more pretentious noble houses.

But there was another part, written down (because it could not be written down) in no book. Though chained at wrists and ankles, they still managed to step along like men and, although beaten and starved, to hold themselves erect like warriors. Their faces were impassive, expressionless, except for the great black eyes, ceaselessly roving about, judging and measuring and surveying everything and everyone around them.

As Wandor and Berek approached the gatehouse, two hard-faced soldiers stepped out into their paths. One of them raised a peremptory hand and asked sharply, "Names and business?"

"Jophal Perkor and Sir Brechal of Tafardos, riding north to seek service against the Khindi bandits," Wandor replied.

"Free lances, eh?" said the soldier. "Can't see as you'll find much fighting up there, not with the Duke bringing the whole garrison down from Fors. Twelve thousand

66

foot and three thousand horses, they tell me. They'll clean out the north woods this summer, then march down here to Yost for the winter and clean out the south woods on the way back to Fors next spring. We've been turning out on extra duty three-four days a week to clear campgrounds and dig privy pits for them."

"The whole royal garrison, you say?" said Wandor.

"Gods help us, yes," replied the soldier. "Those Khindi have been getting too uppity, and——"

Savage cries and the clash of metal interrupted. Wandor spun around in his saddle, to see the line of Plainsmen prisoners coiling like a snake around four or five soldiers, brown wrists reaching up to clutch at their throats or wind chains around them. The other soldiers of the guard were stabbing wildly with javelin and sword into the milling confusion, but even when their blows took effect, the Plainsmen made no sound, but sank silently and stiffly to the ground.

When it was all over two minutes later, and six soldiers and some twenty Plainsmen lay dead on the bloody stones of the street, Wandor turned back to the soldier, who shook his head. "Those Plainsmen'll do that. All of a sudden, a line of them'll get the idea of taking a few of us with them, and then if you're in reach you just hope you're in good with the gods, because they're who you'll be seeing next. I've seen a whole company desert because they were detailed to guard a hundred of those brownskins." He shook his head and turned away as Wandor and Berek spurred their horses through the gate.

They were well clear of the city wall before Wandor spoke again. "Those Plainsmen," he said, and was silent again.

"Yes, Master—about those Plainsmen?"

"I was just thinking. Baron Delvor's daughter, they say, rode over the Silver Mountains to those people when she was fourteen, and was initiated into some rites or other by their Red Seers."

"Do you believe that, Master?"

"That a fourteen-year-old girl could go among those savages and return alive? I could more easily believe a tale that she had gone among a pack of lions and turned them all into house cats."

Wandor's guess about Dogustam was correct enough, and Dogustam's memory for faces was as great as his loyalty

67

to Cragor, so that Baron Galkor had a recognizable description of Wandor within two hours of the time he and Berek passed out of the city. But the Baron, although he had his suspicions, could not be sure that this unusual pair did in fact include the much-sought agent, and he could hardly send his guards and garrison troops hurrying off into the hinterland on a mere suspicion. So he turned back to the stack of papers on his desk, and was just disposing of one dealing with cleaning the main drain from the Yost slaughterhouse when the door crashed open and Kaldmor the Dark came stamping in.

The sorcerer's face was as purple as his robes, and his voice vibrated with barely suppressed fury as he said: "What are you doing?"

"My duty as governor—what else?"

Kaldmor seemed to take a firm grip on his temper, then said, "Your *duty*, my lord Baron, is to carry out Duke Cragor's orders and seize the King's agent, who passed through this city not three hours ago!"

"Oh, you mean that pair Dogustam reported? Are you sure?"

"My knowledge comes from sources quite other and quite more sure than any of yours. I am."

"Then I suggest *you* do something about him, Master Kaldmor. I have no such knowledge, only suspicions, and I will not on mere suspicions——"

"You will not have a head on your sholders much longer, Galkor, if you do not cease to treat me with contempt and disdain. Continue it, and both you and your arrogant master the Duke will feel my fullest displeasure."

Galkor sighed. He had no great use for sorcerers as a group, and still less for this pompous blusterer in the purple robes, regardless of what the peasants might whisper about him in the castle alleys and village streets. On the other hand, if Kaldmor went off to tell the Duke of Galkor's continued ill-treatment, there might be great trouble of the purely natural kind Galkor feared more than any sorcery, and which he believed in avoiding wherever possible.

"Very well, Master Kaldmor. I give you leave, by my authority as governor, to seek out a place to perform whatever rites you need to deal with the man."

Kaldmor nodded sharply. "You begin to have some glimmerings of wisdom. I will take *that* room"—pointing to a door opening off the chamber—"and I order you to let no one enter for twelve full hours. *No one,* I say, no matter what you or anyone else hears or sees or smells or senses. When the door is opened I can promise you the agent will be gone, and perhaps you will have cause to tremble at the thought of what you have risked by provoking me these past weeks." He motioned to his servant, who placed the ebony-faced box inside the room indicated and hastily withdrew, then he stepped inside and pulled the door shut after him.

Inside, he threw the bolt and, having no trust in Galkor, placed a strong locking spell on it. Then he knelt down before the box, opened it, and began to take out its contents.

Four gold pots with crystal lids. A crystal vial of green powder, glowing softly in the dimly lit room. A mummified human hand, brown and grisly. A great white horn with a bronze lid bound on with silvered cord. Five tall black candles in black-iron sockets. A Sthi short sword, its blade silvered and inscribed with golden runes. And the great carved oak staff with gold cap and silver toe.

The casket emptied, he placed it carefully to one side, then stripped to his skin and piled cloak and sandals neatly in the corner.

The five candles he laid out in a pentagram; the green powder he gently sifted along lines stretching from candle to candle. Within the pentagram, he placed a quadrilateral of the four gold pots, then sifted a little of the contents of each on to the floor and mixed them well with the tip of his staff. In the center of the little pile, he placed the hand, and in the hand, tightly grasped, the short sword. Finally he lit all five candles, raised the horn in one hand and the staff in the other, stood in the center of the whole array, and began to chant.

"Earth Walker. Fire Kindler. Water Caster. Air Rider. I, Kaldmor the Dark, call in my need. Come that ye may be fed. Come that I may be served. Come that Toshak may rise again. In the name of Toshak, I call you."

The little pile of mingled powders began to writhe like blankets covering a restless sleeper, and a silver-tinged blue glow began to rise in the chamber. Higher and higher the twisting powders rose, dancing like a dust devil; brighter and brighter the glow. Kaldmor smiled to himself, took a deep breath, and lifted the horn to his lips.

As he pursed them to blow the great call to the Four Spirits of Na-Kaloga to rise up, the blue glow suddenly flickered and danced and flared, then began to fade before a swelling incandescent gold fire that rose up in the chamber like molten rock filling a volcano's pit. The glow became still brighter, and its heart began to show a shimmering, swelling pillar of crimson. Kaldmor shrank away. He had seen that crimson pillar before.

But he did not abandon his struggle. He blew the horn —and instead of the great trumpet blast, there came out a pitiful wheezing and whistling like the death agonies of a slaughtered pig. He dropped the horn, raised both hands high over his head, and shrieked his ultimate word, "NA-KALOGA!"

For a moment, the golden glow shrank, and the crimson pillar dissolved into the fire. Then it swelled again, forming, coalescing—and the last shreds of the blue mist were snatched away by a thunder blast that made the whole palace jump like a startled horse and dislodged plaster and chimneypots all over the city.

Kaldmor landed on his back, and lay there looking up as the crimson pillar finished solidifying—and the Guardian of the Mountain stared coldly out at him. His eyes were icy and furious, and his voice, when he spoke, even more so.

"Kaldmor the Dark. What you do to serve your foul masters, that is between you and them. But you shall do nothing against Wandor. Wandor rides forth under my protection, from you and your kind and your arts."

Kaldmor struggled to his feet and tried to raise his hands, but found them pinioned to his sides as though by steel shackles. His mouth opened, and a croaking sound came forth, "Wandor—is—he—the——?"

"I, the Guardian of the Mountain, do not answer the questions of low crawling things such as you, but bid them crawl away into the darkness and the slime whence they sprang. I so bid you now. Go!" And as the chamber went dark, Kaldmor felt his limbs grow cold and a rushing in his ears as he toppled senseless to the floor.

Baron Galkor was a prudent man, and he therefore waited the full twelve hours. At that point, the locking spell wore off and Galkor's men broke down the door and entered the chamber.

They found it murky with foul-smelling smoke, Kaldmor's box and all its contents reduced to piles of charcoal and puddles of melted glass and metal, and Kaldmor himself stretched out board-stiff on the floor, with only a faint wavering of the smoke before his nostrils to indicate that he was still alive. In the center of the floor, the stone had been melted into a pool of gold-speckled green glass.

Galkor knew little enough about sorcery, but he could recognize disaster and failure when he encountered them. He burst out of the chamber and went leaping down the stairs to the guard room, bawling for soldiers and messengers, and soon riders were thundering out of the city in all directions, galloping madly through the haze into which Wandor and Berek had disappeared a full fifteen hours before.

XI

THROUGH THE DARK rushing grayness of Gwynna's fading dreams flashed a sharp and painful sensation. It shocked her fully awake in an instant; she sat up in bed and concentrated on that part of her senses where the flash had struck. A picture took shape: two men on horses, a tall dark man and an even taller red one, and in their minds the aura of fear. At the very limit of her senses, but growing stronger, was another blurred mass gradually resolving itself into a dozen men riding headlong after the first two, and in their minds murder and destruction. She sprang out of bed and began pulling on her riding clothes.

Wandor knew that the turning to Castle Delvor was barely five miles ahead, but he had little hope they would ever make it before their pursuers came up with them. The men behind them—the retainers of some landowner loyal to Duke Cragor, no doubt—were on fresher horses and they were riding light.

It was a bad situation, but no great surprise—Baron Galkor must have sent messengers thundering in all directions when he learned of their arrival (although how that had been done remained a mystery), and it was at least as great a surprise to have been left free of pursuit so long. Nor was it a hopeless situation, although if the men pursuing them were unusually good fighters, even Wandor and Berek together might go down before their combined assault.

He spurred the horse to a fresh effort, his eyes darting from side to side, looking for a good defensible point to halt and meet their enemies. Nothing—nothing but a wall of giant trees fringed with a tangle of brush along the road.

Uphill they rode, their horses panting and foaming, gravel spraying from under thundering hooves, dust rising in a plume behind them. Wandor fingered his sword hilt, and saw Berek reach back and check the straps that held Thunderstone fixed to his saddlebags.

The road stretched level before them, green-gold in the forest-hued light, then sloped downward slightly. And at the bottom of the slope, a *path* turning off to the left! Wandor gestured frantically toward it; Berek nodded. Both pulled their horses around; Wandor's in a sudden savage burst of energy, reared with a frantic neigh, nearly throwing him from the saddle. He held on, and they plunged into the shadowed path.

It was old and overgrown, moss and leaves and weeds matting its floor thickly and muffling the hoofbeats of their horses. It was dark beneath the trees, but this to Wandor was a virtue—two against twelve would need surprise on their side. He thought of his bow—and then abruptly the path widened a fraction on either side, and the sun poured down straight from high above on to a tiny patch of golden meadow grass speckled with slender blue-green flowers.

Wandor reined in sharply and motioned to Berek. They leaped down from their horses and led them into the trees on the farther side of the clearing, then began to pull their weapons free. The clearing would give them complete freedom of movement, while their pursuers could attack from the path only two or three at a time.

If in fact the pursuers were still on their heels. . . . He and Berek listened. Had they turned into the path before their pursuers came over the rise to see them do so? He had not looked back to see. And if they had—would they be willing to risk a pursuit down the dark path into the forest?

The question was answered a moment later as the sound of hooves suddenly ceased amid shouts and angry cries, and then resumed, muffled and softened but slowly increasing. Wandor drew an arrow from his quiver and nocked it to his bow. At times like this, one of the great Khindi longbows would be a blessing from the gods. But one had to take what they sent. . . .

Fifty yards down the path, a fleeting bit of sunlight flashed on a gilded cuirass and a ruby clasp. Wandor's bow twanged, and the arrow flew straight into the chest of the lead horse.

Horse and rider went down with a crash of armor and cries of pain and fury as the other riders piled up behind their fallen leader. Then the leader was on his feet again, waving his men forward with his sword flashing—until a second arrow sank into his face and he fell.

The first three men at least were brave. They leaped their horses over the body of their leader and came charging headlong down the path and, after a moment spent recovering and remounting, the rest followed. That moment was just enough for Wandor to unleash one more arrow, and see it bounce impotently off the center man's cuirass.

Then the whole thundering pack was coming at him. He dropped his bow, drew his sword, and stepped clear of the trees, Berek behind him. Thunderstone swung howlingly in a flat arc that ended in the chest of the center man's horse. It went down like a falling church, and before its rider had hit the ground, Wandor's blade sank into and through his sword arm. A quick upward thrust ran in under the cuirass of the man on his left, and as he fell, Berek stepped forward to hold that side while Wandor dealt with the third man of the front rank.

This one was a better swordsman than usual, besides having the advantage of being mounted, and by the time he finally ran his point through the man's thigh, Wandor had barely time enough to whirl around and put one throwing knife into the throat of a fourth man before pulling out his dagger and going at the fifth with it to aid his sword.

Blood sprayed over Wandor as Thunderstone sliced down through the collarbone of a man trying to stab Wandor from low on his left, and sparks also sprayed as the great ax's backswing sent another's sword spinning out of his hand. The man leaped back, nearly fell over a root, but recovered, dodged another stroke, and sprinted away down the path.

This sparked a general rush for the road. Wandor dashed for his bow, but before he could launch an arrow, the surviving seven men were all riding back down the path at a wild gallop. He thrust the arrow he had drawn back into the quiver, slung his bow, and ran for his own horse with Berek beside him. They vaulted into their saddles and turned the horse's heads down the path and galloped after the vanished seven.

As they approached the road, Wandor crouched low in his saddle to make a smaller target in case some hardy soul retained the courage to attempt an ambush—and then sat bolt upright in surprise. From the road sounded not one, but *two* sets of hooves—and then both suddenly stopped, and in the silence a high clear voice spoke out, "By what right do Sir Nores Agzor's men pursue fugitives on the land of House Delvor?"

A moment's grumbling, then a single gruff voice, "By what right does House Delvor shelter traitors to the King?"

"To the King, you bitch-whelped cutthroat, or to Duke Cragor?" More grumbling and a few oaths, then Wandor and Berek broke out into the sunlight.

The seven survivors of the pursuing band were spread in a half circle across the road, confronting three well-armed huntsmen in Delvor livery. Between the two groups, a slender youth on a magnificent roan mare glowered at the seven, and as Wandor and Berek appeared, added, "Any traitor to Duke Cragor, we hold a friend to the King, and he has our protection to our last breath."

With four against seven, Wandor thought that last statement perhaps a trifle bold; that last breath might be drawn very shortly if anything went seriously wrong. Perhaps it would be wise to inform this bold lad that he and Berek required no protection that their own swords could not provide. He rode forward and raised his voice: "I am Bertan Wandor, and the quarrel with these men is mine alone. You have no cause——"

The youth stiffened in his saddle. "*I* am——"

"Look out!" roared Wandor. He leaped his horse forward just enough to interpose himself between the youth and the short spear that suddenly snapped out from one of the seven men. The spear struck—sank deep into Wandor's saddle, missed the horse, but laid his own thigh open to the bone.

He gasped and reeled and clapped a hand to the wound, then snatched it away as another rode forward with his sword swinging up to strike at the youth, snatched his own sword free, and drove it into the man's unguarded armpit. Now the youth had his own sword free, and sparks flashed as he parried the clumsy strokes of another, while behind him the three huntsmen snatched out their boarspears and emptied two enemy saddles with them before spurring forward with their short swords flying clear.

Five to four now and then it was five to three as

Berek ran up with Thunderstone swinging and sent it flashing down through cuirass and ribs into the heart of the man fighting the youth. A moment later one of the huntsmen reeled out of the saddle with a knife between his ribs, but his killer followed him down a second later with the youth's sword slashing across his neck. For one moment there was a tangle as the youth blocked the two huntsmen and Wandor blocked Berek, and in that moment the two survivors of the enemy dug in their spurs until their horses reared, then thundered away down the road.

Wandor saw them go and heard their diminishing hoof-pounding through a thickening fog. His head was swimming, he felt his body sway—and then as in a dream he was toppling out of the saddle to fall with a crash, gravel digging into his back. His last memory was of the youth—a pale worried face under a broad-brimmed green hat with a gold feather—bending over him.

XII

WANDOR CAME BACK to consciousness, rising up like a fish through a fading swirl of mist and blackness, until his eyes at last began to pick things out of the surroundings. The first thing was the youth, hatless now, pale face fringed with flaming red hair——

"Great gods above!" he exclaimed. "You're a girl!"

The girl—woman—threw her head back until the sun flashed on her hair and laughed high and clear, then nodded. "I was wondering when you were going to notice it. I'm Gwynna Delvor. Thank you for saving my life. I should have expected such treachery; the gods know we've endured enough of it these past few years." She shook her head again.

"You've lost a lot of blood, but I bound up your wound, so I judge you'll be fit again soon enough. But right now, we'd best be getting back to the castle before any more unwelcome visitors appear. Can you ride?"

Wandor flexed his leg experimentally. "I think so. At least, better than I can walk."

"Good. Then let's mount up."

The six of them—the five living and the dead huntsman slung across his saddle—came up to Castle Delvor from the south. It sprawled across a hilltop that rose out of the forest like a great ship in the sea, curtain wall and bright-windowed hall and squat stables and shops and the great turreted keep with the Delvor banner drooping limply in the still hot air. Their road took them through mile after mile of fields—wheat and oats and barley, rye and turnips and peas, vineyards and orchards—surrounding snug, thatched cottages and barns, surrounded in turn by stout man-high log fences reinforced with stones and earthen embankments. Wandor found the thought of the labor represented by these miles of fences staggering, and said as much to Gwynna.

"The peasants did it of their own will," she replied. "The forests around us are filled with marauders, on four legs and on two, which are best kept from the fields if one wishes a good crop. Granted, we ourselves do benefit. A hundred archers could defend any of these fences against a fair army."

Wandor nodded. He was beginning to see just how well Baron Delvor's loyal service had been repaid. He only hoped that his own contribution would not seem too pitiful amid the forests and fields and the great castle looming higher every moment.

They clattered across the drawbridge and into the castle courtyard. To the left the afternoon sun shimmered on the windows of the Great Hall and the five-towered shrine; to the right part of the court had been walled off, and through the gate in this wall came the shrieks of children playing and the smells of slops and cooking. Ahead were the stables, built along the courtyard wall, and beyond them the keep reared up its hundred feet of gray stone.

Wandor turned in his saddle at the touch of Gwynna's hand on his arm, although the pain made him wince. Two tall, gray-haired men with Knight's emblems were approaching from the direction of the Hall. Wandor's hand went up in salute to the nearer of the two.

"Honor and greetings, my lord. I am Master Bertan Wandor of the Order of Duelists, sent to your House by His Sacred Majesty——"

"Master Wandor!" said the man severely. "Your honor and greetings should be directed first to the Baron himself." He gestured in the direction of the other man, who smiled gravely and bowed slightly in acceptance. Wandor added, "I fear a wound sustained in my journey here makes it somewhat difficult for me to pay my proper respects, but——"

"You are wounded?" exclaimed the Baron. "But of course—I should have seen the blood! Sir Gar, summon a litter and bearers and the priest and the herbwoman and the steward with fresh bandages and food and wine and——"

Gwynna's peals of laughter interrupted him in mid-flight. He looked severely at her; she looked unblushingly back at him and said, "Father, please. He's not dying— it's only a spear gash in the thigh, and I salved and bound it myself. But he will need the litter."

The Baron nodded. "Well and good. But how did you en——" before a warning cough from Gwynna, echoed by a considerably louder one from Sir Gar, reminded the Baron that perhaps not all of Wandor's adventures—or Gwynna's—were fit for public discussion. He cleared his throat, bowed to Wandor, who returned the bow as best he could, and strode away, leaving Sir Gar to deal with the situation.

This the seneschal did with such vigor and despatch that half an hour later Wandor was stretched out on a couch brought up from Sir Gar's chamber into the trophy room, his wounded leg propped up on cushions brought from Gwynna's chamber and bound up with a fresh bandage steeped in herbs brewed by the priest and herbwoman. The void in his middle was rapidly filling with pork pasty and cheese and onions and strong yellow wine. They had taken his clothes, caked and stained with blood and sweat and dust, and bathed him from head to foot before clothing him in a fresh woolen robe.

Wandor had been received in a number of noble houses in his years as a Duelist, although it was more usually members of the Order of Merchants who hired champions from the Order to settle their disputes by combat. He could recall none so well kept and well served as Castle Delvor. Much of this, he suspected, was to the credit of Sir Gar, who was even now standing silent and gray like a sentinel by the door.

Not so the Baron. He lolled back in a richly carved and gilded chair, his thick-fingered hands toying with a cup of red wine—wine much the same color as his face, Wandor noticed. His manner to Wandor was that of one experienced fighter and man of the world to another, with no tinge of condescension. Wandor recalled to mind what his old tutor in arms had said of the Marches. . . .

"Out there, there are indeed lords and peasants, as there are everywhere by the laws of Alfod the Judge, but lord or peasant, a man is judged by what he has in him." And the old man had added with a wry grin. "They can't afford to do it any other way—they're a handful of men holding a thin line against the darkness."

The Baron drained his cup, cleared his throat, and said,

"Master Wandor, for your sake I much regret your wound. But you need have no concern for ours. What Duke Cragor may be planning against us will not come to ripeness until long after you are fit and well again. So you need not hurry your recovery beyond reason—and I suspect with Gwynna nursing you, you will feel no desire to, either."

Wandor felt himself flushing, then smiled thinly—thinly, because he was not so sure of Cragor's sloth. The guard at Yost had spoken of the royal garrison coming south under pretext of dealing with the Khindi bands. He stirred, and was about to speak, when Gwynna entered.

She had also bathed and changed her clothes, and as she stalked in, her blue robe swirling about her, except where it clung, Wandor wondered how he could ever have mistaken her for anything male. He managed a contortion of his torso that passed for a bow; Gwynna returned it, and settled herself gracefully into a chair placed for her by Sir Gar.

The Baron leaned forward and said, "Now that you're here, daughter, perhaps we can learn of what happened this morning to give Master Wandor his wound." He nodded to Gwynna. "You first, daughter."

"I felt an urge to go for a ride this morning, so I gathered up three of my huntsmen and we were riding north along the High Road when I saw seven men burst out of the path that leads to Golden Pond. They were wearing the livery of Sir Nores Agzor, so I thought fit to inquire what they were doing on our land, and their leader said they were pursuing a traitor, so I——"

The Baron raised his hand. "Their leader? Not Sir Nores himself?"

"No. Master Wandor and his servant Berek slew five of the men pursuing him along the path, and——"

It was now Wandor's turn to raise a hand. "Was Sir Nores a tall ginger-bearded man accustomed to wearing a gilded cuirass and a black cloak with a ruby clasp?"

The Baron nodded slowly.

"Then he was the first one I killed. He and his men had been pursuing me from early in the morning, so——"

"Great gods above deliver us!" roared the Baron. "A knight—a sworn vassal of Duke Cragor—slain on my land by a royal agent coming to me! And his men with him." He shuddered. "Go on, daughter. There is more?"

"I asked what sort of traitor he meant—to the King or

to the Duke, and I said that enemies of the Duke would always be welcome as friends of the King"—the Baron groaned and even Sir Gar frowned—"and at that point Master Wandor and Berek rode out of the path after the seven and"—she looked at Wandor—"there was a second fight, in which my huntsman Jacdo was killed, and five of the seven also. They——"

The Baron interrupted again. "Two got away. Wounded?"

"No."

Sir Gar could not repress a groan; the Baron's bellow made the dishes rattle and jump. "You fools! You pair of prize fatted idiots! First this swashbuckling duelist kills Sir Nores, and then you tell his men that we will shelter the Duke's enemies and then you *both* bungle it so that two of them get away to carry the word of all this to the Duke himself! Why didn't you get down on your knees and give them a petition to attack us?"

Gwynna started to rise. "Father——"

"Enough! All gods, what did I do to deserve this? Why did you let my Gwynna, my own daughter—why let her rob me of my last chance for a decent death?"

Gwynna bounced to her feet, her face nearly the same color as her hair, her voice shaking. "*I* robbed you of that chance? What chance did you ever have, once you'd decided to honor King Nond and fight for him instead of joining all the lapdogs and fools in bowing down to Duke Cragor? You cast yourself into this, Father, and I honored you for it and I honor you still. Perhaps now you'll see why we have to——"

"NO!" The Baron surged to his feet and stood over his daughter, shaking his fists. "*No Plainsmen.* Never, never—never while I breathe. I will never bring those murdering cutthroats across the mountains just because you swallowed some myth that witch Zakonta fed you along with her foul drugs! I will die as a Knight with my men around me—not pandering to a horde of naked barbarians on horseback!"

"Then by all the gods there are three fools in this room, and the third the greatest of them!" shouted Gwynna. "Is there nothing to make you see? Do I have to——?"

"If you ride one pace toward South Pass, so help me all the gods, Gwynna, I'll have you locked in the keep until your wits come back. And if this—Duelist"—he made the word sound like an obscenity—"lifts a finger to help you, I don't care if he's the Grand Master of the whole cursed Order, I'll have his head." He lunged for Gwynna's wrist, at the same time turning his head to glare at Wandor.

Gwynna tore herself free, stared at Wandor for a moment, then burst into tears and ran out of the room. The Baron sent another glare at Wandor, turned away, and followed his daughter. Sir Gar sighed deeply, gave Wandor a final look—long and searching, but not hostile—and followed his master out.

XIII

WANDOR'S WOUNDS healed slowly but uneventfully, as did the atmosphere in the castle. By the time the priest and herbwoman decided it was safe for him to walk, the Baron no longer glared or snarled at him every time they met. Sir Gar would occasionally come by to talk of old battles and the affairs of House Delvor, and Gwynna. . . .

Although he saw her every day, sometimes in the morning, clad in her hunting costume and riding out with her leopards, sometimes in the evening, regally graceful in a blue or silver or bronze gown, there remained something about her he could not understand. Very simply, he did not desire her.

The Order did not demand celibacy, and few of its members practiced it—certainly not Wandor, a lusty man of twenty-eight. And Gwynna, he knew, was fully twenty, ripe—exquisitely ripe, as any man with eyes could see—to be transformed from a girl into a woman. Wandor's mind saw and understood, but no hint of this fact ever reached his body.

The Order *did* demand honorable behavior toward those one served, and seducing the daughter of one's employer was strongly disapproved. But instead of succeeding in preserving his honor (and Gwynna's) only by heroic self-control, Wandor found himself unable even to contemplate taking Gwynna. This he did not find pleasant; he found it even less pleasant that he had no slightest notion of how this reluctance arose.

It was not that Gwynna was avoiding him. It was not that she was shy or retiring in manner; she hunted and rode and shot her bow like a man, and with men, and without a trace of strain or effort. It was not her clothing; she put off her hunting costume in the evenings, and her gowns were in almost the latest style, with a display of neck and shoulders and breast enough to awaken any man's senses. And it was not—a thousand times not—that she was not beautiful. It was not from anything in her or about her or that she did or did not do. It was as though some force outside either of them had risen up between them, and shut them off from one another.

Wandor was contemplating this and other mysteries in his room one evening after dinner when a knock on the door heralded the arrival of the Baron himself. He strode across the room, plopped himself into a chair, loosened his belt a trifle, and smiled somewhat uncertainly at Wandor. Wandor kept his silence. The Baron frowned, licked his lips several times, and finally spoke:

"I—well—I don't think I've been—perhaps—behaving quite like a proper host these past weeks. I'd like to ask you to accept my—apology?" The last word held a questioning note that was almost painful to hear; both the Baron's voice and his color were rising. Wandor smiled back, rose, and clasped the Baron's hand.

That cleared the air somewhat. The Baron rang for wine and settled back into his chair. "Since King Nond seems to have trusted you enough to send you, he must have faith in your judgment. He doesn't trust easily. I sometimes wonder how he was persuaded to choose you sight unseen. But now that you're here, and healing, well, it's time to find you a post. I need a good man to head the scouts . . . would that be to your taste?"

"Would I be any good without knowing the land, sir? And remember, it would take months to learn my way around, and Duke Cragor may strike any week."

The Baron shook his head. "Not without his whole army, and we needn't fear anything less." The last was said with an air of bravado—Wandor wondered what he had done or said to make the Baron think he was stupid enough to swallow this story. "Sir Festan Jalgath's too good a soldier to let the royal garrison be sent into a campaign in the Marches with winter coming on; without the royal regulars, all of Cragor's allies between them would be swallowed up in the forests and spat out in little pieces." Again the note of bravado striking completely false on Wandor's ears. "So we'll have ample time to make you a first-class scout, and anything else that may come your way."

The wine arrived; the Baron emptied one cup and began another before speaking again. "Master Wandor, you've heard of how Gwynna went across the Silver Mountains to the Plainsmen, and received some sort of 'initiation' from their witches?"

"From their Red Seers, yes," said Wandor.

"Personally," the Baron went on, taking several deep breaths, "I don't believe she ever did any such thing. I think it was a little girl's running away, and the whole tale an excuse for being gone." He laughed—a painfully forced laugh. "Anything else you hear are servants' tales, no more." He licked his lips again, while Wandor sat silently.

Finally the Baron went on. "But she seems to believe that she has some—influence, power, whatever—over those savages, and I fear she might try to really ride across the mountains and get herself killed. So what I would really like to have you do is watch her and keep her from doing any such thing. I don't want to lose her, even if she has gone mad in some way, she's all I have left of her mother, all I really have left to live for. Will you promise this—it is the greatest service you could render?"

Wandor held back a number of questions such as "What makes you believe Gwynna will listen to me?" and "Why are you telling me this long tale when you yourself don't believe a word of it?" and sat in polite silence for a moment. As clearly as if someone had spoken, he knew he should promise no such thing. But to refuse what was clearly the Baron's wish, without mortally offending him—how?

A moment more of silence, and then: "My Lord. [Formality always pays well.] When I took my Oath as a member of the Order of Duelists, I swore always to 'hear with my own ears, see with my own eyes, feel with my own hands, taste with my own lips'—to use my own judgment in all things. But I also swore to keep the weak from oppression, whether by the strong or by their own follies, which can often be the greater oppression. Would you not call that enough?"

To judge from the expression on his face, the Baron would not. But he had also enough sense to realize that he would get no more. He nodded slowly, rose, and walked quickly away.

A week later came the day when priest and herbwoman together examined his wounds and smiled and declared them healed. Wandor danced a little at the words. Berek

85

did not dance—it was not the manner of his people—but seemed to walk straighter and lighter.

And after that came day after day in the saddle, exploring the miles of forest and valley and stream and field that made up the Barony and the lands of the Baron's Marcher allies, bringing down game for present feasting and future need, feeling his strength return and his limbs grow quick and supple again. Sometimes he rode with Berek, sometimes with one of the huntsmen, a few times with Gwynna. He still could not break down that barrier to desire, but he had given up wondering about it. It was a mystery that would answer itself in time.

He also felt an increasing chill in the morning and evening airs, and saw the green fading from leaves that soon began to blaze with colors. Autumn was coming on, and they were no closer to finding a way clear of the menace from Cragor.

It was on one of these mornings—early, in the chill blue light of dawn after a night of troubled sleep and formless dreams of weird blue glowings in a shadowy land of woods and hills—that Wandor awoke to hear the Castle filled with shouting and the stamping, neighing, and hoofbeats of horses, metal clashing and doors slamming, men crying out in anger and women in fear—and then his own door crashed opened and the Baron burst in.

His face was pale and his heavy hands could not be pressed together tight enough to keep them from trembling. His words poured out like water from a broken dam.

"Gwynna did not come back last night and now her horse has returned without her and last night there was fire in the hills and she was out there among it and, oh, all the gods have mercy on her and——" At which point he ran out of breath and collapsed into a chair.

Wandor sprang out of bed and began pulling on his "Fire in the hills, my lord? A forest fire?"

"Witch fire, Master Wandor—blue as sapphire, but glowing, glowing like nothing of this earth. A great sheet of it, flickering and flaring along the treetops, lighting them without burning them. The sentries saw it just after midnight and called me. It was to the north—toward the mountains."

Wandor nodded. "Which way did Gwynna ride when she set out yesterday?"

"South—she said she was riding *south*. But she didn't

say she was nighting out, which she always tells me, and now her horse has come back and——"

This time the Baron was interrupted before he could run out of breath by Berek's entry. The huge Sea Folker was fully dressed for the trail and Thunderstone swung in his hands. Wandor looked from Berek's impassive ruddy face to the Baron's frantic one and then spoke sharply.

"Berek, we are riding out in search of the Lady Gwynna." He turned to the Baron. "Was there anything unusual about her, in manner or words, when she left yesterday morning?"

The Baron took several deep breaths to calm himself and considered the question. "No, nothing, unless—wait a moment, yes. She said—she was just mounting up, and she sniffed the air, and she said 'The air will sing to-night.' "

Wandor repeated the phrase to himself, then nodded to Berek. The two men we went out, heading for the stairs, leaving the Baron slumped wearily in his chair.

XIV

WANDOR AND Berek left the castle at a dead gallop, but slowed to a canter as soon as they were out of sight of the keep. They continued on the south road for a mile beyond that, then took the first turning north.

It was toward the north, toward where the witch fire had danced the night before, that Wandor knew he would find Gwynna. Knew it, again, as though someone had spoken it directly to him. And not only Gwynna would be there, but the answers to other questions—who or *what* was she? What was keeping her from arousing desire in him? What did she speak to, out there where the forest broke like a green tide against high gray mountain rock?

They were clear of the Delvor lands before noon, and by mid-afternoon they were mounting the road over the last range of hills before the mountains—the same range where the witch fire had flamed. Wandor found himself looking about nervously, although he knew no merely physical precautions could stand for a moment against the powers that might be, surely were, walking these hills. He forced himself to concentrate on the narrowing road ahead, looking for signs of Gwynna's passage.

They looked until the sun was dipping beneath a rose-tinted horizon, and they looked in vain. They called, with no answer except from the birds and the wind. They rode forward, until the road turned to a path, and the path itself vanished in a wall of forest rapidly darkening as the light faded from the sky. The wind vanished, too, and they sat on their horses in a thick enveloping silence.

Wandor sighed. "We'll not find her blundering around here in the darkness, and we're likely to lose ourselves as well. I think we'd best camp here and go on in the morning. Although if she doesn't want to be found. . . ."

"True, Master. An army could hide in this forest. And if someone else wishes that she be not found. . . ." Wandor did not press Berek to finish the sentence. He himself found the prospect of camping here, surrounded and spied on by the forest and swathed in this brooding stillness, quite unpleasant enough without defining his fears more precisely.

Soon a fire was blazing and its light and cheerful crackling pushed the gloom and silence back enough to ease their nerves a trifle. They ate salt meat and biscuit with their daggers, then Berek settled himself against a tree and motioned Wandor to their blankets. "I will take the first watch, Master. I will wake you at midnight." Wandor was too tired to protest; he rolled himself up and was asleep in seconds.

He woke up without any help, and the first thing he noticed was Berek—sound asleep, snoring heavily, and toppled over on the ground. The second thing he noticed was that the fire was out. Not only out, but not even smoldering. The third thing he noticed was that the darkness seemed thicker than ever. He took a deep breath and coughed violently. He licked his lips—and grimaced at the acrid taste. He reached out a hand, and then rubbed it hastily on his breeches.

All around him the darkness clung, a thick damp coiling mist, foul to the taste and smell and slimy to the touch. He thought of fire, and listened carefully. The silence was still all around them. He stepped forward a pace—and jumped sharply as a branch cracked underfoot. He stood still, and around him the darkness flowed thicker and thicker; the shallow breaths he took filled his lungs with foul odors.

On top of the keep at Castle Delvor, one sentry nudged his companion and pointed with a trembling finger. "Look —over there to the north."

They looked. North toward the mountains, the stars marched down toward the horizon in regular procession, then abruptly vanished behind a vast black curtain suddenly sprung out of the hills. As the men watched, it coiled and swelled and climbed higher and higher, blotting out the stars one by one—and as the cloud climbed, they turned with one thought and one motion and dashed down the stairs to the guard room, voices rasping with terror.

It seemed to Wandor that the darkness around him was turning almost liquid and that his last breath was only a few moments away. Then he felt a whispering of air on his cheek, and the murk began to flow—he could *feel* it flowing, sinking down steadily into the earth about his feet. His breath came normally now; he raised his head to look for the treetops looming out against the stars once more.

He never saw the stars, for the treetops suddenly burst forth with a blue-white glare that made him cry out and clap his hands over his eyes. Gradually he raised his hands, gazing in awe at the branches tossing madly in the windless air, tossing and flaring like torches without heat or smell of fire, burning diamond-bright.

He turned slowly, raising his hands to pray for—if not mercy, at least understanding—from whatever powers of the Ancient Days now loose in these lonely woods. The Five Gods would have no power here.

The earth heaved under him; the trees danced still more wildly. His head spun and his knees buckled and he fell heavily to the earth. He rose to his hands and knees, looked up—and saw Gwynna.

The blue fire spread its light across the miles, and in Castle Delvor bells rang and gabbled prayers rose into the air as a thousand men and women went to their knees and called on the gods for mercy or cursed them for their sloth. On the wall, the Baron closed his eyes and pressed his forehead against the stone and gasped, "The fire again! And Wandor and Berek now! What is it? *Whose* is it? Will it never stop? Will it take us all? Is it Cragor's sorcerer calling up his Power?" He groaned and shivered, then cried, "Gwynna! The gods forgive me for driving you to this! My little Gwynna!"

Gwynna stepped out of the forest. She was nude, and the pulsing blue fire made her white body a flowing, dancing vision. Her hair—Wandor gasped and for a moment turned his head away in sheer horror and disbelief—gods deliver him, her hair was *glowing,* glowing bright with an inner fire of its own, casting an incandescent molten glow over shoulders and breast. She raised her arms and beckoned to him.

He rose and followed. His body was no longer his own, or was it? Deep within it, a familiar sensation was stirring, pulsing and flaring like the witch fire itself, and he knew that now it was Gwynna arousing it, and only Gwynna, the Gwynna who danced before him, each motion flowing effortlessly into the next, leading him on and on.

They came out of the forest again, into a clearing where man-tall ferns marched down to a shimmering green pool, making a canopy high over a bed of golden moss. Gwynna stopped and it seemed that her body stiffened for a moment, then she fell forward.

He caught her before her knees touched the ground. His arms went around her, pressing her body close against his own, until her own strong supple arms lifted. He felt her hands moving over his own body, pulling the clothing from it, and then the velvet moss against his skin as they slipped down and her sleek body, soft over steel muscles, melted into his and her arms came around his back and locked them together. . . .

XV

THIS TIME Wandor was awakened by the sound of bare
feet padding softly across the moss near his head, and the
first thing he saw was Gwynna leaning over him. A most
agreeable sight she was, for she wore no more than she
had worn the night before (less was impossible). She
smiled to see him awake, then flowed down into a sitting
position and clasped her hands around her knees.

Wandor cautiously sat up and shook his head. He felt
quite good, surprisingly enough. He looked around. The
ferns, the moss, the pool—all there, even though they
looked a trifle different in the normal light of day. He
found there were two thoughts dominating his mind—one,
the obvious one, rising up whenever he looked at Gwynna;
the other, a sense of emptiness in his middle.

"Is there anything to eat around here—wherever this
is?"

She laughed. "Fire is forbidden [By whom? he thought]
but we can have fruit and nuts and mushrooms and——"

"So why do we sit around with our stomachs rumbling?"

They breakfasted as she had promised, using fern leaves
as plates and napkins together, and carrying the seeds and
skins and stems to a small hillock where a black hole gaped
in the moss. After that, she pointed to the pool and sug-
gested a swim.

The pool was deeper than Wandor cared to imagine and
icy cold. But it cleared the last fog of sleep and uncertainty
from Wandor's mind. And Gwynna, laughing and giggling
as she rose up from below to duck him, or diving, sleek
and graceful as an otter, from the bank, the water beading
her skin and. plastering her hair down around her temples

and over her back and shoulders—she looked even more desirable than ever. It showed plainly in his eyes, so the next time that she popped out of the water, she rolled up on to the bank and lay back on the moss with a smile flickering on her face until he joined her.

A very long time after that, they heard the neighing of horses and bushes cracking and Berek's voice thundering, "Master! Master!" and then "Where are you, Master?" Gwynna wriggled so much trying to keep from laughing out loud that she had to hold on to Wandor to keep from rolling into the pool. And again, it was a very long time before he let go of her or she of him.

Finally Wandor lay back, with Gwynna curled against his chest, looked up at the sky, and said quietly, "We'd best be getting up and on our way. We've the best part of a day's ride back to the castle." She nodded, rose to her feet, and vanished among the ferns to reappear a few minutes later in her hunting clothes. Wandor pulled on his own, then, hand in hand, they climbed up the slope toward where Wandor had left Berek and the horses.

With Wandor's horse having to carry double, they made slow progress, and it was well into the afternoon before they were clear of the winding path and on the road to the south. And it was not until he felt himself no longer overheard by the forest that Wandor dared to deliver himself of a few simple questions.

"Gwynna. Who are you—or *what* are you?"

He felt the body pressed against his back stiffen, and heard a small stifled noise. When she spoke, her voice was toneless and low.

"Six years ago there was a night when witch fire also danced in the hills and the Earth Voices called me. I mounted up and rode over the mountains to the Plainsmen. They took me before Zaknota, Red Seer of the Gray Mares; she taught me the seer-trance and what may be learned while in it. And she also said this: 'Gwynna Firehair [it was Wandor's turn now to stiffen]—guide yourself henceforth by the Earth Voices. They will shield you from the desire of all men until One comes. That One, you shall yield yourself up to him, to give and gain joy in the yielding. And when this is done, bring him to me for his Testing by our Law, by our Rule, by our Book.' "

Wandor reined in his horse and turned to stare at

Gwynna. "Bring *me*—to her—for a Testing—by—their Book? What book do these horsefolk follow, tell me?"

"The Seer Book. It contains many thing, including Tests for all needs."

"And *this* Testing?"

"That only Zakonta herself can tell you."

"And Zakonta is of course on the other side of the mountains, perhaps a month's ride out on the plains, and winter is coming on. Do you truly expect me to ride out there on the strength of such a—*story?*"

"Yes."

"By what right, may I ask? Remember we will have to deceive and evade your father and perhaps Sir Gar and certainly all the sentries; if we fail you will certainly be for the keep and I perhaps for the block. And then we have to get through South Pass without being caught by the fort's garrison of better than two thousand regular soldiers who are almost certainly in Cragor's pay. And then we have to find one woman—or at least, one tribe—out of all the Plainsmen, in all those endless miles of grass and sky. And then I am to be thrown head-first into the gods know what kind of Testing for the gods—and perhaps you and Zakonta—know what purpose." He snorted. "Do I look that sort of a fool?"

Gwynna's body suddenly went taut and rigid, and, before he could stop her, she leaped to the ground and stood there shaking her fists at him.

"You *are* a fool. We don't go through South Pass, we go through one three hundred miles to the north that practically nobody except the neighboring tribes knows about. And the Plainsmen will be going south to their winter pastures along the northern edge of the Blue Forest, so we won't have to ride all over the Plains the way you think.

"And as for my right—the Earth Voices kept me a maiden for six years—through years when girls my age had children old enough to run. Then they gave me to you, and gave you desire so that you would take me. And you took me, and you gloried in it and so did I. Our shared love gives me that right, and yet you sit there and ask where it comes from!" She turned sharply and sat down on a stump, her stone-stiff back turned to Wandor.

Wandor had enough experience of women to understand that he would never understand them. He signaled to Berek, who dismounted from his horse and tethered it to a bush, and did the same himself. Then he walked over to

94

a spot off to Gwynna's left and just outside her field of vision, pulled his boots off, and lay back on the grass. It was as soft as a feather mattress; shortly he found himself growing drowsy. This was not surprising; very little of the night had been spent in sleeping. But he could not afford to sleep; they had to move on to reach the castle by nightfall. He hoped Gwynna's anger would soon pass.

After a while, he noticed that Gwynna had not moved for several minutes. Her back was as stiff as before and her arms were now crossed tightly on her breast. He rose and walked around to look at her face—and sprang back with a gasp of sheer horror.

Gwynna's eyes were blank pools of shimmering green, swirling and dancing like the witch fire of the hills. Her body was rigid as a tree trunk, yet vibrating softly like a plucked harpstring. And her hair—once again her hair was glowing in the twilight of the woods like iron over a forge.

He felt his limbs becoming as stiff as Gwynna's, but he forced himself to take one, two, three steps toward her. As his shadow fell across her face, her clenched lips parted in a terrible rasping shriek, and she jerked to her feet, arms dancing woodenly like those of an ill-made and worse-handled puppet. Gradually their thrashing slowed until they hung rigidly at her side. She stood there for a moment in a silence broken only by Wandor's quick breathing, then her lips opened again and she began to speak. It was not her voice; it was another woman's—deep and rich and vibrant with power to command.

"Bertan Wandor. I, Zakonta, Red Seer of the Gray Mares, call you. I call you in proof of the truth of Gwynna's tale, which you seem to doubt in spite of all that has passed. Doubt it no more. It is the truth. She is bidden to come with you over the mountains, bringing you to us for your Testing. Swear now, by all that you hold sacred, and by the Earth Voices that guide us all, that you will come."

Wandor went down on his knees, largely because they would no longer support him, and shakily raised his hands and voice to swear a solemn oath by the Earth Voices, by the Five Gods, and by his own honor as a House Master of the Order of the Duelists. He managed to keep his voice steady, but toward the end he could no longer keep his eyes fixed on Gwynna's writhing and contorted features.

Suddenly there was silence, followed by a long whistling

gasp as all the air seemed to rush out of Gwynna's lungs at once and she sagged to the ground. Wandor scooped her up before she fell and held her in his arms, close to him, while she shook and sobbed and clung to him and his own tears of relief flowed down to mix with hers.

It was long after dark when they finally came in sight of Castle Delvor, but they could easily make out the line of torches along the distant battlements. The Baron was waiting for them, or perhaps lighting those torches simply to drive away whatever might choose to walk about tonight. If that was his purpose, Wandor reflected, what pitiful means he was using!

He turned to Gwynna. "How soon should we plan on leaving?"

"I don't know how long we can keep my father placated," she replied. "So as soon as possible. Also, winter is supposed to be coming early this year, and if we want to cross the Zephas before the autumn floods———"

Wandor shook his head. "All this is true, but we are going to stir not one foot for at least a week. The past three days have been an ordeal for you at least as great as my wound was for me. To tell the truth, you look sick."

She sighed. "You *will* insist on being protective. Very well. One week. But not a day longer—if nothing else, game becomes scarce on the northern plains, and we can't possibly carry enough food for the whole journey on just two horses."

Wandor nodded. "I'll remember that. But now—let's agree on a story to tell your father, and see if we can't keep him ignorant of our real intentions until we are ready to ride out."

XVI

Duke Cragor was in a grim mood when he rode into Yost with the advance guard of the royal garrison—a thousand heavy cavalry and five hundred mounted light infantry. The weather had been foul when he left Fors, and it became steadily worse as they marched south. The bottom dropped out of the road, the men fell ill with fevers from the endless damp and the cold rations, and every few miles progress came to a complete standstill while they laboriously hacked their way through fallen trees or rebuilt bridges washed out of existence by the rains.

The Khindi were the worst of all. Every time the column stopped, and even at times when it was on the march, sooner or later a savage "Ki-i-i-i-yah!" would slash through the rain and fog, followed by anything from a half-dozen to three-score arrows, bringing down men and horses and draft oxen amid screams and bellows of rage. And there was nothing to do about it; the handful of royal archers could never have matched the range of the great Khindi longbows, even with dry bowstrings. In this dismal weather, they were helpless against the Khindi with their resin-coated bowstrings.

It was not only the attacks on the troops that bothered Cragor; the Khindi seemed to be more active this fall than for some years. Reports from farther inland told of cattle lifted whole herds at a time, horses hamstrung, barns burned (or looted and their contents distributed among the local peasantry), ambushes and waylayings, even the burning of a few weakly defended manor houses. And all of it *outside* the Marches—though it was in the Marches that the Khindi bands were said to cluster thickest. This might be a coincidence—Delvor and his supporters would certainly not wish to report widespread Khindi raids and give Cragor or one of his supporters an excuse to move against them—but again, it might not be. Cragor made a mental note to have the matter thoroughly investigated.

Coincidence or not, it would cause him trouble. Some of his most reliable allies might become unwilling to send their men away on a prolonged campaign, leaving them defenseless. He would have to promise a short, sharp, victorious war to keep them faithful to him. And Sir Festan would insist on keeping thousands of regulars tied up in castle garrisons, and he would have to be humored if he were not to understand the true motive for Cragor's "campaign against the Khindi."

If Cragor had been in a foul mood when he reached Yost, what he learned when he reached the Governor's Palace and spoke to Baron Galkor and Kaldmor the Dark made it even worse. The Baron, claiming as his excuse the insecurity of the roads, had carefully avoided mentioning the disasters that had followed in Wandor's wake, and naturally Cragor had assumed silence gave proof of success.

And equally naturally, he was livid with fury to discover that this silence had concealed total failure and disaster. This was not pleasant hearing for the Black Duke, and he reacted accordingly.

When the windows had stopped rattling in their frames, Cragor turned to Kaldmor and snapped, "May I inquire, Master Kaldmor, for what reason you were unable to exercise your widely heralded and loudly boasted powers against this solitary Duelist and his companion? Your explanation had best be a good one, or by the time you have thought of another, you will have no tongue with which to utter it."

Galkor looked nervously at the sorcerer. Wise men did *not* talk to black sorcerers this way—at least not more than once or twice. But Kaldmor actually seemed ill-at-ease, if not actually frightened—and that was a most agreeable sight. Galkor grinned inwardly. Whatever had happened in there that night when Kaldmor had puffed himself up so much, only to wind up flat on the floor of that stinking chamber, it had chastened the man. More power to whoever had done it!

Kaldmor er-ed and ah-ed and muttered into his beard until Cragor's expression began to darken again, then said,

"I did my best, my lord. But this Wandor—he is not whom I thought he was. He is——"

"Of course. He's not a mere Master Duelist; he's really the long-dead great-aunt of His Sacred Majesty King Nond come back to life. You've made a poor enough start; let's see if you can be as lame and halt in the rest of your story." Cragor dropped into a chair, ostentatiously crossing arms and legs and pursing his lips.

Kaldmor swore out loud in several languages, then exploded, "Duke Cragor! If you regard my failure as giving you license to make sport of me, you will pay for it sooner or later. I tell you, Wandor is not what he seems. He has a—protector, whose name I cannot mention to you—and it was by the work of this protector that I was prevented from dealing with him as I had intended. That he has this protector proves——"

"That you are not as powerful as you have claimed? Quite possibly. But why *cannot* you tell us the name of this protector? Are you *forbidden*? If you serve no masters as you have said, then who forbids you? Or rather, *what* forbids you, except perhaps fear of admitting your own foolish arrogance and swollen vanity?"

Kaldmor glared at the Duke, his arrogance and rage now matching Cragor's own. *"I am forbidden*—and you would be wise to press the matter no further, or the answers may be displeasing. But that Wandor has this protector proves he is important far beyond our previous imaginings, and dangerous to us—to you—far beyond your greatest fears. We must move against him at once, against him and all who support him!"

Cragor looked coldly at the sorcerer. "We? And what can you contribute, if you are prevented from acting against Wandor by his mysterious protector? Can you be sure that this protector will not casually extend his invincible protection to Baron Delvor and his household as well, and even to the Lady Gwynna—although to be sure, I forgot, you yourself said that she can call up the powers of the Plainsmen Red Seers in her defense and Wandor's?"

Kaldmor shrugged. "From what I know of this protector, he is unlikely to extend his protection and aid to others than Wandor himself. But I cannot be sure. On the other hand, can you be sure that your own confidence in the swords and bows and knives of your allies will not prove equally misplaced?"

Cragor spat. "They can hardly accomplish *less* than your

arts have, or seem likely to. And now—to our real plans. A message to Sir Festan, ordering him to move the royal garrison south as fast as possible, by forced marches if necessary. We must have it here in case Delvor decides to take the offensive this fall. Other messages to all our allies within two days' easy ride of the south Marches. They are to call up all their mounted men and all the foot soldiers they can find horses for and move into the south Marches and burn as many crops and as much food and as many houses and farms as possible. If we can drive the peasants and yeomen to shelter at Castle Delvor or the Baron's allies, a horde of useless mouths will consume much of their stored food and make a siege unnecessary, after we destroy their fighting men in the spring. Our friends are not to worry about the Khindi; any losses they may suffer will be made up out of confiscations from Delvor and his allies."

"Confiscations?" asked Galkor. "That means proclaiming Delvor a traitor. Under what pretext?"

"A few real ones and many rumored. As for the real ones—his daughter slew, or helped to slay, Sir Nores Agzor and his men—a loyal and honorable knight. His daughter out of her own mouth stands guilty of conspiring against me, another loyal and honorable man. And there are rumors—or will be soon enough—of alliances with the Khindi, the bandits, and even the Plainsmen. *That* should drive the waverers screaming terror-stricken into our arms."

"The alliance with the Plainsmen may in the end be more than rumor," said Kaldmor quietly. "A week ago I sensed for two nights together the Earth Voices openly speaking in the hills north of Castle Delvor, and the day after that second night there was such a great disturbance in the web of the spirit world as might be made by the Plainsmen seers. If the Lady Gwynna was at work. . . ."

Cragor nodded. "Then all the more reason for haste. Have parties sent out to bring in as much salt meat and preserved vegetables as possible for the use of the troops this winter, and have them do so before the farmers get wind of our need and start hiding their food or doubling their prices. Offer a fair price but be merciless with hoarders and concealers. And, Baron Galkor, have you a really *good* daggerman in your household, or must I use one of my own?"

"My Lord Duke?"

"It has occurred to me that it might be worthwhile attempting the assassination of our friend Baron Oman Delvor. I much dislike having to give him such a quick death; he deserves a more thorough treatment. But if we can shorten his years by whatever means come to hand, it might shorten our fight for the Viceroyalty."

XVII

THE MIST THAT had clung about them ever since they started down from the pass was as thick as ever when Wandor awoke. He felt stiff all over, and cold, except for the side against which Gwynna lay, snuggled up like a kitten. Up here there was no point in keeping a watch—the mist and the dark would keep a man's hand invisible when held in front of his nose. But this coming night they would be down among the mountain tribes, and these tribes were not overly friendly to strangers.

He sat up and looked around. Gods, but he wished he could see the sun! It had vanished with sunset the day they crossed the pass. He remembered the golden disk burning down out of a piercing blue sky on to a waste of rock speckled with patches of hardy grass, on to the distant peaks flanking the pass. In the crystal-bright chill air, the peaks seemed to loom near enough to touch. Every crevice and ridge stood out, as did the gleaming fields of snow on all the level patches. A month early, Gwynna had said, and her face had been hard and set and frowning for hours afterward.

That night, rain fell from sundown to what he guessed might be sunrise. Mist all day, rain that night, mist the next day—and so on. The rocks were slimy-slick with wetness and the damp chill clawed its way through cloaks and coats and boots.

He would have felt better with Berek along, or would he? Another man to guard their backs, true, but he would find plenty to do at Castle Delvor. And in any case Gwynna had been adamant. "The Plainsmen kill strangers on sight, even more since their experience with the slavers.

I am known well enough to secure the safety of one companion, but not two. And there are things in the Testings which no outlander may see, at least none not bidden to come."

And without Berek, Wandor felt freer with Gwynna. The trek was no romantic interlude and Wandor, not being a fool, did not seek to convert it into such. But to learn more about this fascinating creature—to come to know not only the exquisite soft over-supple body, but the spirit dwelling within the body and all the fancies and delights dwelling within that spirit—this could not fail to proceed better with the two of them alone.

The thought made him look down at Gwynna. As if the thought had been a touch, she stirred, stretching catlike as her green eyes blazed open and stared up into his.

"Morning, love," he said. "Time to move."

She nodded and sat up.

They rode side by side down the slope, letting their horses feel a sure way among the stones and gravel. As they rode, they talked, mostly of the Plainsmen—or the Yhangi, to call them by their proper name.

Gwynna was firm on one subject.

"They're not barbarians. They don't go naked, except into battle. And they aren't even completely horsemen, at least not in the wintertime."

"What do they do in the winter?"

"The Plainsmen live off the great elk herds of the plains, and when winter comes, each tribe drives its herds south to the edge of the Blue Forest, where there remains grass for them all year round. They make their camps, feast, hold marriages and manhood rites and sacrifices; the Council comes together to award guardianship of the King Horse——"

"King Horse?"

"To the Plainsmen, the horse is sacred. They may not eat its flesh; they may kill a wounded horse only with a consecrated knife. Their chief god is man-bodied and horse-headed; his dwelling place on earth is in the King Horse that no man may ride. Each year the Council of the Yhangi—the Speakers, War Chiefs, and Red Seers of the twelve tribes—meet at Council House and honor the tribe that has best served the whole people by awarding them the guardianship of the King Horse for the coming year. The tribe so honored is regarded as the most favored by the god, who guides the judgment of the Council. For the last two years, the Gray Mares have guarded the King Horse, because of Jos-Pran's leadership in breaking up the slaving rings operating among the Blue Forest towns."

Wandor nodded. "Plainsmen slaves have become a fashion among the noble houses who can afford them. A stupid custom, for it takes three free servants all their time to keep a Plainsman slave from killing either himself or everybody else within reach. But I know of nobles who have paid two thousand gold crowns for a Plainsman *woman*—and mortgaged manors for a man."

Gwynna laughed bitterly. "Of course. There is nothing those bloated peacocks of the higher nobility won't do if it's the fashion. But of course, Duke Cragor saw that if he could secure a monopoly of the supply of Plainsman slaves——"

"It would be as good as a private gold mine."

"Or better. So seven years ago he began to send teams of his best man-catchers and soldiers into the towns along the northern edge of the Blue Forest. These towns were once frontier posts for the empire that ruled the Blue Forest in the last century before the Years of Darkness; some say the empire did much to bring those years on. But the towns were built strong, and they have good walls manned by good soldiers.

"They do not live well; they sell salt and metalwork and tanned leather to the Plainsmen in return for hides and skins and meat, so naturally they were not unwilling to share in Cragor's gold mine by sheltering his slavers and even joining the raiding parties."

"How long did the mine last?"

"Five years. Then Jos-Pran, a young warrior of the Gray Mares, had his wife and two children caught by the slavers. He led his clan against the band, but his family was killed before he could rescue them. So he went back north, swearing vengeance, and the next year he was chosen War Chief of the Gray Mares. He led them south— thirty thousand warriors—and stormed two of the towns in spite of all the defenses they could muster and sacked and burned them and put all of their people to death. The other towns then killed or drove out Cragor's slave-catchers, so there has been peace along the forest edge since, and great honor for the Gray Mares and their War Chief."

They rode in silence for some minutes, while Wandor

turned the picture of the Plainsmen over in his mind. Twelve tribes, one at least mustering thirty thousand warriors. He tried to imagine the thundering sea of horsemen the Plainsmen must make assembled together. And they made war without mercy? No wonder the Baron had been frightened of the idea of bringing them into the Viceroyalty to fight his enemies! An alliance with the wolves or the sharks or the vipers would have been as useful, and hardly more dangerous.

Gwynna must have noticed the expression on his face, because she laid a hand on his arm and said in a gently chiding tone, "Don't believe the Plainsmen always fight like that. Among themselves, they fight for honor, for women, and for herds; but their greatest mark of valor is to defeat a strong enemy without killing him. That is one of Jos-Pran's great boasts—to have bested in eight years forty-one opponents, killing only three. But as for strangers and, above all, those regarded as enemies of their people, they show no mercy to them except a quick death."

Wandor decided to let the matter drop; there would be time and opportunity enough soon to judge the Plainsmen for himself. Instead, he said, "For now, I'm more worried about the mountain tribes between us and the Zephas. You say they are unfriendly to strangers?"

"Only in defense of their flocks and homes. Small parties such as ours often pass through their lands and are ignored as if they were invisible. And at this time of year the tribes withdraw into their cave homes and drink and feast and make love and seldom come out into the wet. We're in far more danger from the autumn rains than from the tribes."

They rode on. Wandor found himself torn between annoyance that a woman of twenty should be so calm and knowledgeable and self-possessed, and so given to reassuring him in an almost motherly fashion, and prayers of gratitude that it was so. Gwynna's self-possession and quick mind made her a far safer companion on this rugged journey—and made her no less delightful at other times.

Gwynna was right about the mountain tribes ignoring them. Occasionally gaunt skin-clad figures would materialize from the mist-hung forest and stand silently amid the dripping branches, staring at them from under shaggy brown hair for a few moments before vanishing whence they had come. The rest of the time, the forests seemed as

105

empty and sullen and apparently lifeless as the mountains now falling behind them.

The rain and the mist kept alternating all during the five days it took them to ride clear of the forest, and this bothered Wandor partly because the food and fodder they carried in their saddlebags might spoil in the constant wet, partly because it was so obviously bothering Gwynna. She would not tell him what it was, but every morning when she rose up from his arms and saw the sky leaden and dripping as before, her face set a little harder and the lines on her forehead deepened a little more.

The day came when the forest began to thin out, and they rode for hours with only a few clusters of stunted pines to break up the monotony of the scenery. All the streams they crossed were filled to overflowing, boiling down the slopes with an urgent grumbling and gurgling, carrying twigs and the bodies of small animals in a steady stream. The horses began to wheeze and labor; the wetness was getting to their lungs. Gwynna's face never relaxed now, not even at the climaxes of their love.

And finally one morning the mist lifted, and they rode past a final cluster of pines out into the open, where a pale sun was shining off the wet grass and the pools of water for the first time in weeks. They dismounted to spare the weary horses and let them find what little grass they could, and looked south.

In the distance gray clouds flowed down to a gray-green horizon, flat and level and featureless as a tabletop, with an echoing voice of endless lonely distances coming to them in the faint piping of the wind. The plains.

But between them and that awesome horizon, a vast silver-gray sheet of water swirled and flowed and, in the center, boiled and flickered white around half-submerged trees. Three miles it stretched from where it lapped ankle-deep at their feet to where it seemed to end on the other side. Three miles of rushing water, where Gwynna had predicted a quarter of a mile with a good ford.

She sighed. "This is what I've been afraid of. The Zephas is in flood worse than ever before. And downstream it will simply get wider, so there's nothing to be gained by trying a crossing lower down."

Wandor nodded. "And the horses will be getting weaker and weaker, unless we can get across to the grass of the southern plains. And even we ourselves will be getting hungry soon enough; we have five days unspoiled bread at most. So I'm afraid we've nothing to do but go forward."

Gwynna looked around the landscape desperately. "What about a raft?"

"What is there to build it with around here? Or tie it together? And what do we cut the trees down with even if we can find any? And how long do you think it would take to build a raft strong enough to carry us and our horses together?" He sighed and looked at the water again. "We'd best rearrange the loads, so we won't lose everything vital if one of the horses does go down. And then we'd better start, just in case the weather decides to change again."

XVIII

THE THIN MAN dropped down from the windowledge to the stone floor. His bare feet made no sound, but he stiffened just the same, close-cropped head cocked and ears and eyes intent for any sound or motion in the dark hall. None. He allowed himself a small sigh. He was safe and undetected inside Castle Delvor. Now to find the Baron and accomplish the task Baron Galkor had set him. He had no thought for the man whose life he had been sent to end; only for the freedom and the thousand crowns and the woman promised him if he did it.

In the trophy room, Sir Gar Stendor rose to his feet and looked at the Baron for a moment, shaking his head sadly. Something had gone out of his lord's soul the morning a servant had come running in with Gwynna's note shaking in his hand and the air had been smoking with the Baron's curses and shaken with his anguished cries. Perhaps some other shock would make the Baron rise up and take steps for his defense—and perhaps it would only drive him further into himself. Meanwhile, Sir Gar knew that any slackening on his own part would mean the end of everything. He picked up his cloak and strode out, heading toward the stairs leading down to the Great Hall.

The man padded across the hall, darting glances from side to side. As before, silence. Then he flattened against the wall as booted feet sounded on the stairs, the sound floating through the half-opened door. A shadow fell across the wedge of pale light on the floor; the man took three quick steps and crouched down behind the long oak table. The door creaked wider.

Sir Gar had just pushed the door to the Great Hall open when he realized that he had accidentally picked up the Baron's cloak, blue with a gold border and a diamond clasp, instead of his own plain unbordered green. He shook his head and fingered his beard. Was *he* beginning to break under the strain and the loneliness or was it just age finally creeping up on him? Not surprising if it were the latter, for there had been gray in his beard when Gwynna was born. Gwynna! What had the gods wrought in that girl? Would he ever know all of it? Probably not, but he knew enough—had known it for years—to keep his heart hidden. He turned, and strode toward the stairs.

The light in the stairwell lit up the figure—tall, gray-haired, with a long gray beard—he was fingering it now—slightly stooping, high leather boots and a blue cloak with a gold border—yes, there was the Baron's diamond clasp flashing in the light. It was the Baron, sure enough. As the figure turned, the man behind the table stepped out on to the floor, drew both his long daggers, and darted forward.

Sir Gar heard the footsteps behind him only a split second before the first dagger drove into his body, but in that split second he turned far enough to spoil the killer's aim. The dagger seared across his ribs, and as the man raised the second dagger, Sir Gar drew his own and lashed out. The man leaped to one side, and his foot came darting up, sinking into the seneschal's stomach. The breath swept out of Sir Gar in a single desperate cry, then an even sharper pain burst in his chest. He felt his legs going; his arms darted out convulsively and clutched a greasy leather coat and trousers. He tightened his grip and drew in with his last strength. Now his eyes were going the way of his legs; as he sank to the floor amid gathering darkness, pounding feet sounded in his ears. Through that darkness, Gwynna's face swam up into his sight, steadied, and beside it was Wandor's. The look in their eyes told Sir Gar everything. "I'm glad you found him, Gwynna," he murmured.

Thanks to Sir Gar's death-grip on him, the assassin was held for the few seconds the guards and Berek needed to come pouring out of their quarters and seize him. And thanks to the Baron's coming down the stairs at a dead run immediately after that, the assassin was not immediately sent to join Sir Gar, but was bound and hauled like a sack of grain down to the cellars for questioning. His screams were audible all over the castle, until he finally collapsed. By that time Baron Delvor knew two things: that he himself had been the intended target, with Sir Gar's death the result of accident, and that Cragor was behind the attempt.

"Both of which things," he muttered after the executioner left, "we could have guessed for ourselves. For all we've learned from that wretch, we might as well have given him food and wine and wenches and the run of the castle! But I don't suppose this is the only string to Cragor's bow. I'd best have the guards doubled and tighten up the scouts on the northern roads. Gwynna . . . Gwynna, why did you take yourself off over the Mountains on your mad quest when you were the only person other than Sir Gar I could really trust?"

Although the Baron tried to keep word of Sir Gar's death from leaving the castle, it must have done so in some way, although in the end this was unquestionably for the best. But meanwhile, the castle's inhabitants, from the Baron down to the kitchenboys, walked with one hand on their daggers and one eye always flickering behind them.

One clear but chill morning, the Baron was awakened by the alarm gong, and three heartbeats later several sets of fists began thundering on the door of his chamber. Even after the servant opened it, and the master-at-arms and the falconer and the cellarer and several others poured into the room and began howling around him like wolves around a stag, it was several minutes before he could make it out that they were all shouting "The Khindi! The Khindi!"

"Ten thousand fiends fly away with you all!" he bellowed. "What about the Khindi?"

"They're all around the castle!"

"You can see them behind every tree!"

"Ten thousand of them in war dress!"

"They've captured Sir Gilas Lanor!"

"One of their war chiefs is carrying Sir Gilas's banner!"

The last bits of news snapped the Baron wide awake. Sir Gilas Lanor was his staunchest ally among the northern Marcher lords, and led a stout and formidable band of warriors in spite of being only twenty-four. His capture by the Khindi, for whatever reason, would be a major blow to the Baron's strength. And this on top of Sir Gar's death! The Baron's face was drawn and gray as he pulled on his clothes and, as an afterthought, a shirt of mail over them.

Ten minutes later he was on the castle wall, staring intently into the woods where the swarms and hordes of Khindi were said to be lurking. Age had not impaired his vision, but still, he saw nothing, and he was beginning to wonder if all the panic had been the result of someone's nightmare after too many mutton pasties. Then suddenly the bushes at the edge of the cleared grass around the moat parted, and three figures stepped out into the open.

One of them was indeed a Khindi war chief in full battle regalia, and he was indeed carrying Sir Gilas's banner—black wolf on a silver field. But the second was Sir Gilas's chief huntsman, in full hunting gear plus a Khindi long-bow, and the third was Sir Gilas himself, his impish tanned face peering out from under the unmistakable black helmet with its silver plume. There was a short bow and quiver slung on his back, a sword and dagger at his belt, and a cuirass on his chest—any figure less like a prisoner would be hard to imagine.

The Baron laughed for the first time in weeks. "All right, men. You can spare your sweat and fear for some occasion that really demands them. I don't know what Sir Gilas is here for, particularly with this mass of Khindi, but he's obviously no prisoner. Master-at-arms, go down and have him brought in to my chambers, and his Khindi friend, too."

Baron Delvor drained his wine, his third cup, and again stared at Sir Gilas. Then he poured himself a fourth cup and stared at the knight's companion.

The Khindi chief, tall, yellow-brown, and hook-nosed like all his race, sat calmly cross-legged on the bearskin before the fireplace. His silver-inlaid warbow and quiver of blue-feathered arrows and his scale-mail shirt were laid carefully in a corner. He was wearing only his leather leggings and moccasins and the sleeveless wool undertunic. His long-fingered muscular hands lay clasped quietly over his knees, but the slanting gray eyes were never still, flickering constantly around the room.

The Baron put his cup down untasted and said slowly, "So you've made an *alliance* with these—people?"

111

"Nothing written down," replied Sir Gilas briskly. "Nothing to compromise me—or you, if you want to join us—but we've sworn an oath that my enemies shall be theirs, and my friends theirs, and of course the other way round. For the moment, though, I've more enemies than they do so I have their promise of up to five thousand warriors to serve me here in the Marches at my call."

"Five thousand? My men said you brought ten thousand."

The Khindi chief stirred and smiled slowly. "We have much skill to make few look like many—here be two thousand warriors only."

The Baron shook his head. "I find it hard to reconcile an alliance with these people with a Knight's honor, but——"

"Damn a Knight's honor!" snapped Sir Gilas. "You've your back to the wall, and yet you refuse the only helping hand you're likely to have offered you. You've lost Sir Gar—it was when I heard that I resolved to come over to offer aid—you've lost that Duelist the King sent you and you've even lost your daughter. And Duke Cragor certainly isn't going to limit himself to one attempt on your life. His main army may be three weeks' march away in Yost, but what of his allies? They're many of them within two days of the March borders, and what if he sends them over to start burning people out of their farms and manors? Can you feed the whole March here at Castle Delvor and still stand a siege in the spring? Can you, my lord?"

"No, but I can't risk turning the wavering landowners against me by an alliance with——"

"And why not? And do you think they won't turn against you in any case if they see the peasants and yeomen and even knights who've turned to you for protection harried out of their homes and driven through the winter forests by Cragor's henchmen and mercenaries? But if you join us, and every bush along the northern and western frontier of the Marches hides a Khindi archer, we can swallow every man and horse Cragor can send against us and spit the pieces back in his ugly face. At least, we can do this as long as the Khindi remain with us."

"True enough, but I have obligations as——"

"You have above all obligations as the leader of the men loyal to His Sacred Majesty here in the Viceroyalty. If you go down because you insist on bowing to your Knight's honor when you should be rising up and embracing whoever offers himself as an ally, that honor of yours may cost King Nond his throne! Your friend King Nond!" The young Knight dropped angrily into his chair and sat there stiff and sullen.

Baron Delvor did not take kindly to being told his duty in such terms by a man less than half his age. But regardless of who told him, once he saw his duty he would cleave to it. So after a few minutes he turned to Sir Gilas and the Khindi chief and nodded slowly in assent.

After Baron Delvor had been admitted to the oath, the Khindi chief murmured a polite honorific formula and excused himself, leaving the two Knights sitting and staring at each other and the fire. Sir Gilas broke the silence.

"What is this I hear about Gwynna running away with that Duelist King Nond sent you?" His tone sobered quickly as he noticed the expression in the Baron's eyes. "I'm sorry; you know I offered twice for Gwynna."

"Yes, and I rejected you both times because you would have tried to cage and tame her as she may never be. No, I wish it were simply a lovers' escapade. They are riding across the mountains, to seek out the Plainsmen and bring them here to us as allies in our fight with Cragor."

Sir Gilas shuddered. "I hardly know whether to wish them success or failure. But I can at least hope they survive their journey. We live closer to the mountains than you do, and the oldsters of my villages say they've never seen a wetter or colder autumn. The rains will have the Zephas running high, and when winter comes and the blizzards come riding out of the mountains and across the plains. . . ."

XIX

WANDOR LOOKED from the miles of water ahead of them to Gwynna and back to the water. "Ready, love?"

"Ready."

They urged their horses forward, and the muddy water splashed up around the stirrups. The footing was not quite as bad as Wandor had feared; the horses slithered to the right or the left every minute or so, and once Gwynna's stumbled and went to its knees, dousing her and her gear with brown water, but they kept moving steadily forward, letting the horses feel their path.

"How far before we have to start swimming them?" asked Wandor when they had come perhaps half a mile. The water was up to his horse's knees and above the knees of Gwynna's horse. And the mist was closing in again. Gray woolen walls were shutting out even the dead flat horizon of the flooded plain and dreary tufts were drifting past, thicker and thicker.

Gwynna wiped the water from her eyes and looked ahead into the mist. "About this far again, if I remember how the land lies. It starts sloping down toward the river-bank where the road runs between a clump of fir and an old ruined tower, of Ancient Days work." She peered ahead again. "We should be seeing them soon, if we are on the road and not wandering in circles."

That was a pleasant thought. As it struck Wandor, the mist seemed suddenly to thicken and the lapping of the water around them became more insistent, hungrier. He sighed and dug his knees into the horse's ribs. It whinnied in mild protest and started off again. And the water rose and rose. . . .

114

They came upon the tower suddenly, for the mist was now thick about them, and it loomed out of the swirling grayness, seeming to lean threateningly toward them. Empty windows stared down at them like the eyesockets of a skull; crumbling moss-grown stones showed the water-marks of floods that had risen even higher than the one they were now struggling through. Dark and silent and utterly dead and alone, the tower seemed to Wandor a refuge for the demons that must surely be hovering over this watery desert, waiting to snatch up the souls of men and beasts.

He looked off to the right. There were the firs. And there was the beginning of the slope; the water lapped at the very foot of the firs, but fifty yards farther on two graceful birches stood half-submerged. He thought of the mile-long swim ahead, across the mist-stifled waters, then put the thought away and nodded to Gwynna. They lowered themselves out of the saddle into the water, which rose already above Wandor's waist, and up to Gwynna's breast, and as the faint current tugged at them, they tied leather thongs to their wrists and then to the saddles. If they stayed with the horses they might win through; without them, they faced death through drowning or a slower death from starvation on the other side even if they reached it. Again he nodded to Gwynna—words used breath better saved for other uses—and they urged the horses forward. The animals balked and shuddered and whickered softly, but at last plunged forward; their feet left the ground, and they were swimming forward into the gloom, their riders trailing alongside.

They had covered what Wandor, guessing (what else could one do in this blankness?), estimated at half the distance, when he felt the current begin to tug at him more strongly, and saw the twigs and clumps of grass and the bodies of drowned animals begin to slide past more swiftly. He looked to Gwynna, who raised fatigue-glazed eyes and muttered, "The main current. Till now we've been in eddies and backwaters—the hills make them. But soon now. . . ."

The current took them, whirling the horses around until their heads were pointed downstream, whipping the riders about in the water until their bones creaked and the water lashed over mouths and noses and they choked and gasped and struggled for air that rasped in their throats. Wandor managed to raise his free arm and point. "We've got to get

115

across—across!" and heard Gwynna give a half-choked assent. He hauled as hard as he could on the horse's head with both hands, and the animal thrashed and neighed and tossed its head and lunged it at Wandor. And then it plunged around in a half circle and thrashed ahead. Gwynna did the same, and as her horse turned, she lifted her head and for the first time in hours a faint smile flickered across her dripping face. They were angling across the current now, past wide patches of dirty foam, clods of earth and grass the size of a man, the horses panting and arching their necks and the water leaping over their backs as over half-submerged rocks.

It happened in a split-second. The tree trunk was two men thick and twenty men long, with a mass of jutting branches stabbing forward like the longpikes of a line of infantry. The branches came surging out of the mist and caught Gwynna's horse, lifting it—and her—like a lamb in the claws of an eagle. The horse screamed once wildly, with a dreadful bubbling note as the branch stubs drove through ribs and flanks into its vitals. Then it toppled to one side, rolling over until its legs were half out of the water, as the tree pushed it down and under.

Wandor lost sight of Gwynna for a moment in the flurry of water, and for another moment after that the bottom seemed to fall out of his stomach. He wanted to be sick. Instead he clamped his jaw even more tightly, drew his knife, and slashed at the thong about his wrist. It parted, and he and the horse swept apart as he kicked and thrashed frantically toward the tree. As he reached out his hand for the farthest-extended branch, Gwynna's head rose up from beneath the water, eyes wide and staring white, features slack, hair streaming in the water. He hooked an arm around the branch and with his other arm felt underwater.

Gwynna's wrist thong had snapped, but the loose end was wrapped tight around a branch. He tried to snatch it loose one-handed, missed, tried both hands, and was nearly swept off the tree. Finally he got both knees around another branch, ducked under, and hacked at leather and wood until Gwynna suddenly floated free and he had to drop the knife and grab her around the waist with both hands before the current could sweep them apart.

By the mercy of the gods, his horse had turned downstream the minute he cut loose from it, so it was only some ten yards away. He looked at Gwynna—face white, but when he pressed a hand under her ribs he could detect a faint rising and falling—then crossed her hands over his chest, swung her around until she was riding between his shoulders like a backsack, and struck out for his horse.

They almost didn't reach it. Kick as he might, the gap between himself and what little safety the horse represented seemed hardly to close at all. With his breath burning in his throat, he thrashed out with one arm. His body surged forward the last two feet, the other arm clutched the saddle, and Gwynna rolled off his back and began to drift away. His free arm reached out, fingers clawing, caught her by the hair, held her there with the sodden strands parting one by one and his finger and wrist joints screaming—until the second when he was sure that if her hair didn't pull out his fingers would. And then a sudden eddying long enough by seconds to permit him to shift his grip to Gwynna's collar and gently, slowly but steadily, haul her in until she was firmly clasped with his free arm around her waist, while the other arm gripped the saddle as the horse puffed and struggled on toward the far shore.

How long it took them to reach it, Wandor never knew, but they did reach it, and very suddenly. One moment they were struggling through apparently endless foaming brown water, and the next the horse was heaving itself on to its legs. A few paces farther on, Wandor could put his own feet down on what could pass for solid ground, although with every step he took a stickiness and sliminess seized his feet and tried to hold him back. Not long after that the water sank to the horse's knees, and it was then that Wandor hoisted Gwynna up into the saddle and tied her in place as best he could. And after that he went up to the horse's head and took the bridle to lead it gently forward toward dry ground, where they could stop and dry themselves and see how much the flood had left them.

What the flood had left them, as Wandor found when he had a chance to examine the bags, was more than he had dared hope but less than they really needed. They still had the tent, but only one blanket between them. They still had the wallet of iron-hard trail biscuits, but only one bow and one bowstring and perhaps a dozen arrows (if their fletching had survived) to bring down game when the biscuits were gone. They still had the firekit, but of the firepaste to set fire to the soaked grass and brush they might find, only a single half-empty vial. The prospect of making the trek south on a diet of trail biscuits and raw meat was nothing to view with great joy.

Whatever awaited them on the trek, Wandor knew they might not live to begin it if they did not at once warm and dry themselves. He drove the tent poles into the ground and raised the tent, laid the ground cloth, and carried Gwynna inside, wrapping her snugly in the blanket. Then he lit a fire, with grass and twigs coated with fire-paste for kindling it, and piling on larger sticks when the blaze was going well. Finally he made sure the horse was tethered securely within reach of edible grass, pulled off his own clothes, wrapped himself in them, and lay down besides Gwynna. She was breathing slowly and softly but regularly, and her soft breathing was the last thing he heard as he also fell asleep.

In the morning—another gray morning, but now only clouds overhead, no mist or rain, and a brisk wind whipping the water off the grass—Wandor found Gwynna curled against him in the position that already seemed a lifelong habit. This he took as a good sign, and so it proved, when she opened her eyes, stretched, yawned, curled and uncurled each limb individually, and said, "When do we ride?"

He looked her over, a pleasant thing to do, as always, although the fatigue of the long ride was beginning to grind her down to muscle and sinew, and replied with a question of his own. "When will you feel ready?"

"It's not a question of when I feel ready, its a question of when we *have* to march. With one of us on foot, we'll move more slowly than we could both mounted. That means three weeks to the southern camps, at least—perhaps more, because we'll be having to stop and hunt once we reach the winter grazing grounds of the wild herds." She looked up at the clouds streaming past before the crisp wind. "From what I was told of this wind—the *cholkh*, Zakonta called it—we will have snow within a few days." She unwrapped herself from the blankets and began dressing.

It took them five minutes to bolt down a biscuit apiece, another ten to lash all the gear in place on Wandor's horse. Gwynna mounted up; Wandor took a firm grip on the saddle, and they moved forward across the endless level plain of dying grass that lay before them. And behind them the wind muttered to itself, and occasionally rose to a moan.

XX

BARON DELVOR was inspecting a picket post along the western border of his lands that morning. It was another of the many tasks he had hoped, once, to leave to Wandor and Gwynna; this was another moment when he felt his loss keenly.

There was nothing about the men to surprise him. They looked cold, wet, tired, and exceedingly bored. But he had to make some comment, and so he was riding along the line of horse and foot drawn up before him when there was a *halloing* and a pounding of hooves in the distance. Berek rode crashing through the bushes and into the clearing.

Without dismounting, he called out: "Sire! Sir Gilas reports a hundred footmen burning Pencharg, and three hundred horse on the High Road heading for the castle! And the village bailiff at Copura has sounded the alarm horns, but sent no word of what or who is attacking him."

"And Sir Gilas is doing—what?"

Berek frowned at the acid in the Baron's voice, and replied: "The camp west of Nalkos has been warned; the Khindi and the horsemen there are moving to block the road north from Pencharg. Fifty horsemen have been sent into Copura; they are to deal with that which may be there, including the bailiff if he proves to have sounded a false alarm."

"And the Castle?"

"My Lord, Sir Gilas sends respects and proposes you come see with your own eyes what he has prepared for the castle. He says you will find it heartening."

Castle Delvor was three hours' ride away, but there was

no need for the Baron here, on a yet unthreatened border —and to see something heartening, he would have ridden for three days, not three hours. He jerked his head in dismissal at the picket, and spurred his horse after Berek.

Before they had covered two thirds of the distance, the Baron knew that Sir Gilas's plans included no attempt to stop the High Road raiders much short of the castle. On the horizon, spiraling up from behind the trees, columns of smoke marked the passage of the enemy, gray swirling clouds rising as regularly as milestones and each marking a cottage, barn, or stable that would shelter neither man nor beast that winter. The Baron glared futilely at the spectacle, uttering prayers to the gods and curses on the head of Sir Gilas, and dug his spurs in deeper.

The road they were on forked a few miles from the castle, with one fork running straight into the castle from the west and the other running farther south to meet the High Road. The Baron came up to the fork at a canter— and nearly fell from his saddle, as his horse reared up in fright at a dozen Khindi archers that suddenly sprang up out of the bushes beside the road.

They were in full war gear, and their leader carried the bronze-inlaid bow of a clan war chief. This man motioned to his followers, and they fell into line behind the Baron's horse and followed him south.

They did not have to follow him far, only a few more minutes' ride down the road to within a mile of where it joined the High Road. There he saw a now familiar lithe figure leaning against a tree, gazing off down the road with an air of unconcern the Baron found utterly maddening from the first moment he saw it.

He rode up to Sir Gilas and roared: "Sir Knight! How do you find it in you to stand there while those scoundrels"— he waved a hand south toward the smoke clouds—"carry out their purposes? Where are those Khindi I have let you bring into my service at the risk of a charge of high treason?"

"Patience, my lord. They are all along the High Road, which is after all where the principal enemy is to be found. And do not worry—they know how to make woodscraft serve in place of numbers, and they are the best left to walk their own paths in such matters." Sir Gilas's calm insouciance would have further enraged the Baron, except that as he took in breath to reply, three war horns sounded

121

within seconds of one another, all to the south, and far away to the east, toward the castle, two more replied. Sir Gilas motioned toward the Baron's horse. "My lord, I suggest that you mount up and follow me."

From the back of his horse, the Baron could see only the High Road stretching gray and empty in either direction. But the war horns were still sounding in the distance to tell of the enemy's approach. Would he have the wit to understand what was being laid for him, and turn back in time to foil it?

Now, dimly in the distance, a cluster of horsemen appeared. They grew rapidly larger, more appeared behind them, the sound of their hooves swelled and filled the air—and then a single tortured and torturing blast from all the horns sounded from horizon to horizon, and arrows like horizontal rain sleeted out of the forest and into the advancing riders.

A good quarter of the saddles were emptied in the first few seconds. Horses squealed and reared, bodies thudded to the ground, the survivors cursed and brandished their weapons. The whole advancing mass churned and heaved like working dough, as each man sought to wheel his horse without regard for his neighbor. And as they fought to do so, the arrow hail continued, dropping men from their saddles as they tried to turn and face an enemy with neither face nor place nor body.

Eventually they broke, those who were still mounted and even those who could still stagger along on foot, and half an hour after the war horns first sounded the road was empty except for the sprawled bodies of men and horses and the Khindi stalking jackal-like among them in search of loot. Baron Delvor looked at the scene in disgust, and noticed with a certain bitter amusement that Sir Gilas Lanor's face showed nearly the same feelings.

The young knight spat into the littered dead leaves and swore. "Damned freebooters. They'll swear an oath to serve you, well enough, but only to serve you at their pleasure. And their pleasure is to strike, and slay, and loot the bodies and perhaps the homes of the enemy, and then fade away into the forest and you'll never see them again until it pleases them to need no more loot." He spat again. "They killed close on two hundred men here, but if more than fifty of *them* are still within horn-hail tomorrow morning, you can set me up on the Castle wall and use me for an archery target."

Sir Gilas proved a true prophet, the Khindi proved fierce and deadly and mercenary, and the next ten days proved the worst of Baron Delvor's life since the Battle of Volervas thirty-eight years before. All along the March borders, cavalry and mounted foot and even infantry struck and recoiled and struck again. Smoke curled up from woodchoppers' leaky hovels and stout and well-furnished knights' manors alike. Trampling hooves scarred the fields and bleeding bodies cumbered them. Along the roads wound columns of gaunt and ragged men and women and children. They shivered in the chill days and chillier nights, started and paled at the slightest sound, collapsed by the road when the last strength or will left them, scattered like birds when an enemy war party thundered past with swords slashing down and arrows and lances at work, stopped and gazed numb and gray-faced and silent when the Baron's haggard men came hurtling by on yet another endless ride. And they shivered and cringed when a war-clan of Khindi stalked past, or gaped in awe at Berek's gigantic form riding past with Thunderstone's bloodstained blade riding visible and ready behind him.

The Khindi became fewer and fewer as the days past, for as fast as they quenched their thirst for loot, they felt their oath fulfilled and faded like spirits into their native forests. And while they did this, the Baron and Sir Gilas grew saddlesore and gaunt and chilblained as they coursed the roads from one end of the south Marches to the other and back again, slaying two or three foes here, a dozen there, rarely a score or more somewhere else, always leaving some of their own men lying on the ground beside the peasants already sent down to the spirit world. They saw their horses grow thin and starved and their helms dinted and their swords nicked and battered, reeled in the saddle from fatigue and wounds, itched and stank beneath the armor they dared not remove, they and all of their men fighting each like a dozen, but still too few—until at last on the tenth day it ended.

As the Baron and Sir Gilas rode home to a castle now filled with a thousand homeless refugees of all ranks and conditions, they knew they had lost the opening round. Thanks to the Khindi, in part, but thanks even more to the courage and endurance of their own men and the

123

stout-hearted resistance of the peasants, better than a thousand of the enemy's fighting men had gone down. But with them had gone five hundred or more peasants and no fewer than four hundred of their own fighters, including some thirty men of Knight's rank. And Sir Gilas could hold out hope of nothing better for the next year.

"To be sure, the Khindi will flock to our banners again if they have hope of loot. If not, they will stay in the forests and defend their homes. Of course, they may do that anyway; to get them to fight for me at all was a miracle; to get them to march out and face an army of above thirty thousand, such as Cragor will bring south in the spring, is something not all the Five Gods working together could bring to pass. And if Cragor—or Sir Festan —is wise enough to send his light infantry into the woods, we will be doing well to see five Khindi the whole year."

"Yes, and we will have famine long before that, for the peasants have lost the best part of their seed grain and I expect they will have small chance of planting the little left them next spring. Even if we could stand a siege here in the castle——"

"We cannot."

"Indeed. Our only hope is to ride out against Cragor and, with the help of the gods, slay so many of his men before we ourselves become the vultures' banquet that his plots against King Nond may fail for want of hands to accomplish them."

"Against odds of seven to one? My lord, even with the Plainsmen on our side, that would be difficult. As it is——"

"As it is, Sir Gilas, it will *all* be on our shoulders. There will be no Plainsmen. And no Master Wandor. And"— more softly—"no more Gwynna. Never again."

XXI

ACROSS A GRAY ocean whipped into fury by the first gales of winter, up the long cold gray serpent of the Avar with the last fisherman huddling in creaking smoky huts along its banks, high in the great keep of Manga Castle, two men sat in a room. One was King Nond, the other Count Arlor. The King was praising his confidential agent, a thing he did infrequently, and only when amply justified. This time he felt it was.

"You've done exceedingly well from the beginning of this affair," the King said. "You have pursued every path that might give us new knowledge about Master Wandor, and those you have not pursued, you did not pursue only because you are one and not a thousand, such as the Royal Gendarmes whom I cannot use in this matter."

"Hardly, sire, with half of them suborned by Cragor or his agents. Although I wish I could have discovered more—I sometimes felt, particulary with Wandor's old arms teacher and his foster-parents, that there was more about him which they would not tell me. Still, I learned much that the Grand Master left out of his account.

"At least two men I spoke with reported seeing a mighty storm, with the sky full of a burning many-colored glow—like witch fire—in the direction of Mount Pendwyr. And this on the very night that Wandor would have been passing along that stretch of road.

"Also—" But King Nond was not listening. He sat in silence for nearly a minute, his mouth working slowly, his mutterings gradually becoming audible. "Many possible reasons—natural ones, even—still, that pyramid—if he has Sthi blood, he might well be, but does he?" Until Count

Arlor looked at his master so inquiringly that the King finally noticed it and laughed.

"I've always asked you not to trouble me with rumors and legends, so I will do the same by you. But still it is a strange and not altogether welcome thing for a King to find a good and trustworthy agent, and then have to wonder who or what else the man might also be serving."

Arlor shook his head. "One day we shall have to deal with the Grand Master. If he has been concealing this. . . ."

"Perhaps Master Wandor told him none of it. And in any case, until we are secure beyond fear from Duke Cragor, the Order of Duelists should be left alone. They hate the Black Duke so greatly that they must be regarded as one of our staunchest allies. However, our concern at the moment is with one solitary House Master of the Order, of whom we have heard nothing whatever since the bare news of his safe arrival at Castle Delvor."

"Yes, and also of the Lady Gwynna's threats against Cragor, which may force him to open hostilities next spring at the latest, perhaps even this autumn if he has the royal garrison and its commander deep enough in his pocket. That Gwynna! Her temper flames like her hair."

The King frowned. "The Lady Gwynna," he murmured, and then, sharply: "Count Arlor. You are an expert on that bizarre and preposterous sex known as woman—or at least you claim enough success with them to know how they react to a man. Is it possible that Master Wandor and the Lady Gwynna have become in some way, ah, *entangled* with one another?"

The Count shook his head. "Wandor would prove attractive to women, although Duelists often do not concern themselves with such matters. But the Lady Gwynna will never yield to any man who will not accept her for what she is, without any notion of changing her or taming her to his will, and it is a rare man who can approach a woman with no trace of such a notion visible in him. I do not know if Master Wandor is one of those rare ones or not."

He sipped his wine and continued. "Consider also, sire, that it might be to our advantage if they were to become— I use your own word—entangled with one another. There are women who must give their bodies to such a man, and judge how he takes them, before they will give him their trust. I would say the Lady Gwynna is one such, if one can judge the woman of twenty from having met the girl of fourteen.

"If she comes thus to trust Wandor, she may ask his assistance in going to the Plainsmen across the Silver Mountains, into their winter quarters, and seeking their aid. It is said of her that she was not only initiated into their rites at fourteen, but even now communicates with them in some way not of our earth."

The King grunted. "Rumors, legends, *pah!* Since the end of summer I am dying for want of facts, and what do I get, even from you?" He shook his head angrily. "No more. Someone I can trust must cross the ocean and discover as best he can what is happening there. I am half-disarmed without that knowledge."

"You mean me, of course," said the Count with a sigh. "Very well. But I will have to be well disguised, and have some identity that would give me a good reason for a winter crossing of the ocean, unless you propose that I wait until spring."

"Gods forbid! If you wait until the spring sailing season, by the time you reach the Viceroyalty all there will be for you to do is question the survivors, if you are left alive long enough for that. You sail on the first good ship. I have seen you disguised so your own mother would not have known you; that is scarcely a problem. As for an identity, you will be the captain of a mercenary company formerly serving one of the cities to the south, in the Chongan lands, seeking employment for your men in the war that you have heard is rising in the Viceroyalty. That will explain your undeniably warlike appearance, and certainly give you an introduction to some of Cragor's warlords."

In the Viceroyalty itself, there was another room (in, though it was hard to believe, the best inn in Yost), and there sat four men: Duke Cragor, Kaldmor the Dark, Sir Festan Jalgath, and Baron Galkor. It would have been a fairly pleasant gathering even without the excellent wine exacted from the trembling landlord, for the news was good.

'So," said the Duke, "Sir Gar Stendor is dead, even if that fool of an assassin"—with a savage look at Galkor—"bungled his real task. Our allies have moved against the Marches and, while we have lost more than we expected, Baron Delvor and his allies have lost far more than he can afford. The royal garrison is assembled here at Yost, and if I may say so, Sir Festan, it makes a brave sight. With fifteen thousand royal troops and twice that number of our own levies, we will create a host such as the

Viceroyalty has not seen since the days of the Conquest."

"True, my lord," said Sir Festan. "But remember—we shall have to face the Khindi again, and unreliable as they are they can also be truly formidable if they wish to be."

The Duke shugged. "A rather large *if.* And even in all their strength they cannot stand up against an army strong in light infantry, such as ours—the original conquest proved that. If they march out to fight us, they will be butchered, and that will save us the trouble of going into their forest dens and rooting them out like wild boars after we have dealt with the Baron. The Viceroyalty must be left absolutely peaceful."

Sir Festan shook his head. "What of the Plainsmen, my lord? Were a tribe, or even a clan or two, of theirs to come across the Silver Mountains——"

"Sir Festan, let us hear no more of the Plainsmen. They are on their side of the mountains, we on ours. Between us and them stands South Pass, with its wall fort and a garrison of royal troops. Of course, if you wish to dream of the Plainsmen finding some other way over the mountains, such as developing wings, that is your right as a free man of Knightly rank, but do so elsewhere and let it not interfere with your concern for more immediate and pressing tasks. Yes, Master Kaldmor?" For the sorcerer was slumping in his chair with the weary air of a man who hears but finds himself powerless to do anything about it.

"Sir Festan is much the wiser, for he at least allows for the possibility that the Plainsmen *may* come. But we know that Wandor and the Lady Gwynna have not been seen in the south Marches for weeks, we know that all the rumors have them crossing the mountains to seek aid from the Plainsmen, and if you do not know what the Lady Gwynna can do, or what I fear Master Wandor *may* do, then you have heard not even one word of mine these past months and I will not waste my breath repeating them. Together, those two may find ways to cause us much harm."

Cragor snorted. "Together those two will be hewn in pieces by the first Plainsmen they seek out, unless one believes those fantastic stories about a fourteen-year-old girl riding across the Silver Mountains and the like. Assuming, that is, that either of them survives the blizzards long enough to reach the southern plains." As if to punctuate the Duke's remarks, a gust of wind made the windows clatter in their frames and sent the candles flickering.

XXII

THE BLIZZARD had been blowing four days now, although there in the freezing shrieking emptiness, Wandor found his sense of time slipping away little by little. So was his strength, the horse's and Gwynna's.

She was fading the fastest of the three, although not as fast as before he had caught her giving her share of biscuit to the horse. Why the river crossing had done this to her—Gwynna, the hunter and rider, hardened to all weathers—was known only to whatever malignant spirits had contrived it. But her face was thin and pinched and white as the snow driving around them except in the nights when it was red as her hair as she tossed and writhed in a feverish haze of pain. Then the blizzard had come racing down upon them from the north, and at last there was nothing to do but pitch the tent and contrive what warmth they could within its stiffened, ice-crystaled walls while waiting for the wind to die.

Those four days of rest (if you could call the huddling, shivering agony in the tent rest) at least kept Gwynna from sliding any farther down the road to the spirit world. And on the evening of the fourth day, judged by a thickening of the perpetual twilight outside, after a meal or two of their dwindling stock of biscuits, she seemed so far recovered that she talked of going out with the bow to hunt down some meat when the snow stopped in order to leave their remaining biscuit for the horse. That much Wandor accepted; if the horse died, their deaths would soon follow, but the rest of her idea he rejected.

"*You* still need to build your strength before we ride again, far more than I. And I am a good enough hunter to do what we need now. No, enough!" He held her gently in his arms, and presently they both slept.

The blizzard passed beyond them that night, and the morning that greeted them was searing bright and searing cold. Nothing, not even a breath of wind, moved in all the vast frozen white flatness. Cold as it was, seeing the sun rise again made Wandor's spirits rise also, particularly since from its height he judged they could be no more than five days' travel from the southern lands where they might expect to meet the Plainsmen. Even the horse, stiff and cold-benumbed as it was, seemed to respond. Gwynna broke up the remaining biscuits and fed them to it, bit by bit, from a hand withered frighteningly almost to corpse-thinness and corpse-whiteness.

That hand was in Wandor's mind as he mounted and rode slowly away on his hunt. He *had* to find meat, or the fever that had seemingly receded might rise again and sweep her away. At least, he knew that out here he would not be left long to mourn her—cold, or hunger, or Plainsmen lances and arrows would soon send him to join her. Yet he would not accept such a fate for either of them without a fight, and. . . .

What was that silver-gray shape in the distance? It was moving, low and sinuous, along the snow—neither elk nor wolf, too low for the one, too large for the other. Now it was stopping, foreshortening, rising—rising up and up to the height of a mounted man and more. Wandor reined in the horse to watch, to try and guess the nature of this beast, and then suddenly it dropped down low and began to move toward him. This would be almost too easy; the game was coming right into bowshot.

And then the horse neighed in panic and tried to rear but lacked the strength and stumbled and fell, and as Wandor hurled himself clear he suddenly knew what was advancing on them. A silver bear! Driven down from the mountains by hunger, it had scented the horse and now it was charging on its prey. Wandor would have to face alone with bow and knives and sword a creature that weighed more than himself and his horse combined, with forepaws carrying raking claws that could disembowel him at one blow. This was a creature that not even the greatest hunters in the world sought out voluntarily, but rather avoided whenever the gods by some mischance allowed one to cross their paths.

It was within long bow reach now; should he risk an arrow? It would give him an extra chance. If he waited until it was within easy range, he would have one, perhaps two shots, so fast was it coming as the scent of the horse grew stronger. He drew an arrow from the quiver, nocked it to his bow, swung around until he judged the flight would carry it into the rushing monster's chest, took a deep breath, and drew . . . and saw the arrow arch high and descend as he had aimed, burying itself half in the bear's chest. The wounded animal reared up and clawed at the arrow with a bellow of pain and fury, arching its body— and then dropped back on to all fours and leaped forward again, feet moving as fast as before.

Wandor snatched a second arrow free, nocked and aimed —and with a crack like a dry twig, the bow snapped. The arrow dropped dumbly to the snow. Wandor stared at it for a split second, a man seeing a specter of his own death, then drew his sword with one hand and dagger with the other and stepped back to get between the horse and the oncoming bear. If it killed the horse, he and Gwynna were as good as dead anyway, so why not risk everything?

But the bear was not too starved to show cunning. Thirty paces off it stopped, reared up on its hind legs again —rising up twice the height of a tall man—and let out a long tearing growl. The horse whinnied in panic and bolted. Before it had covered twenty paces, the bear charged across the snow and brought one steel-clawed paw down like a headsmen's ax on the horse's neck. The blow snapped the spine like a carrot and brought the horse to its knees. Before it had finished falling, the bear sank teeth and claws into its flanks.

For a moment, the hunger-crazed bear left its entire side open to Wandor. He sprang forward, thrusting with his sword, and saw the point go in deep, felt it grate on bone— and then felt it wrenched out of his grasp with a force that almost broke his wrist as the maddened bear sprang up and struck at him. The clawtips of one paw laid open chin and lips and left cheek to the bone; a few inches deeper and the paw would have split his head like a rotten melon. He lunged forward desperately; the paws came down again, closing like the jaws of a nutcracker, the bone in his left arm snapped. And then as flesh and skin ripped away from his right one and the bear's open jaws flashed full of blood-stained white fangs within a foot of his own face, he drove the long dagger through fur and and skin and between the

131

ribs and into the heart. The bear toppled to one side—had it fallen forward it might have been the victor, even in death—twitched twice and lay still.

Wandor looked at it dimly until his head cleared a trifle. He felt that he would like to lie down and join the bear, and he knew that if he did not get back to the tent as fast as his legs would carry him, he would do so. One arm broken, the other laid open halfway to the bone—no hope of cutting off meat from either horse or bear, not even any hope of drawing his dagger from the body. His face was a mask of blood from nose to chin (he could feel it stiffening in the cold except where his lips kept it a salty slime). Go. How much time to the tent? And how much time after that before his wounds and her fever and cold and hunger made an end for both of them?

He never knew the answer to the first question, because he never knew how far or fast he traveled until the moment when the peaked shape of the tent swam up out of the glaring snowfield. The second moment was when the flap stirred and Gwynna crawled out, rising to her feet with a motion so like the bear's to Wandor's befuddled mind that he reeled back, staggered, and fell. Her face froze in horror as she saw him, then she reached down and grasped him around the chest. Wandor heard her joints creak as the full strain of his own two hundred pounds came on them; he churned the snow with his feet and managed to rise and stagger into the tent before falling flat on his back, the whole world dancing slowly about him.

She wrapped him in the blanket, splinted his broken arm with three of the arrows, and bandaged his other arm with strips torn from his breechcloth. She then piled his blood-caked and filthy hunting tunic and breeches on top of the blanket to add some slight warmth. Then she crawled out on to the snow, stood up, and without a word began to take off her clothes.

Wandor rose up off the tent floor with a lurch, until the agony in his arms made him drop back. He gasped, "Gwynna! Have you gone mad!"

She turned with her tunic half over her head, drew it entirely off, and stared at him for a moment. "I must do it this way if I am to call up the Earth Voices, to send a message for aid to the Plainsmen."

"But your fever?"

"If I send no message, we will both die, fever or no. Let

me be—this is *my* knowledge!" Wandor lay back and watched her as she finished undressing and stood, nude and white as the snows around them, her hair flaming against the sky. Slowly she knelt twice, keeping her upper body perfectly rigid, then sprang erect and stood still and stiff as a pillar of ice, the infinitely slow rising and falling of her breasts the only sign of life.

Wandor forgot his own pain in the thought of what she must be suffering standing there, sick and weak and starved and every inch of her exposed to the frigid air, motionless and silent out on the snow. He watched her, for she was still a beautiful thing to see—in his eyes, he knew she always would be—and if she fell, perhaps he could bring her to safety.

She neither fell nor moved, nor did anything move anywhere in the vast white snowscape. At last he saw a slight tremor of her knees, then her lips quivered and she collapsed on to all fours and crawled hastily into the tent. She was shaking all over. And even without looking at her, simply by running his hand over her bare back, Wandor could feel the fever again burning in her.

"The Voices came," she gasped. "But the Plainsmen—I don't know. No one answered. Zakonta . . . where is she?" Wandor managed to reach out his better arm far enough to close the tent flap, stretch out the blanket to cover her, and then lie back with her head on his chest. It seemed a good enough position in which to die, and Wandor, though Master Duelists were brought up to die hard, knew there was little or nothing else left to do.

When he awoke from a dream where Gwynna's face and swirling golden fires with tall crimson figures coalescing out of them, and long sunlit paths through green forests all danced in confusion, it was dark and a thin piping wind blew around the tent and trickled icily in through the flaps. He licked his dry lips and looked down at Gwynna.

There was still a trace of warmth in her body; otherwise he would have called her dead. She was motionless and limp, eyes staring sightlessly; when he called her name, not even the fluttering of an eyelid indicated a response. He sighed. It seemed a strange thing to worry about, here and now—but he did not want her to die now, not until he was ready, so he would not have to lie here in this frozen wilderness alone. But perhaps he could will himself to sleep, and so pass to join her faster.

133

He roamed through his memories, and recalled a day on the great white sand beaches stretching for a day's ride north of Tafardos. There had been a girl, but somehow Gwynna's face and body—gleaming and sun-spangled, her hair curling down over shoulders and full high breasts—had slipped into the girl's place. They ran naked through the curling foam on the green water, and like dolphins plunged into the deeper water and dove and surfaced and dove and surfaced again until the beach was far distant, then rode the waves slowly back again, letting the waves rock their bodies against each other as desire swelled up within them. Then they could stand again. They ran up the beach to lie down in each other's arms on the pine needles carpeting the dunes just inshore from the beach. As their bodies merged, Wandor felt a vague *frustration*—his mind was too fogged to rise beyond that—that what he had found with Gwynna should be so short. Then as the warmth of her body and the warmth of the sun and the sand enveloped him, with dim traces of cold and darkness hovering around the edges, he slowly sank into silence and pleasure and utter peace.

XXIII

INTO THAT PEACE, filled with warmth and bright but fading colors, intruded a sudden succession of aliens. Wandor heard horses neighing, low voices, a blast of cold air, and finally a face. It was a Plainsman face, and Wandor muttered resentfully at its intrusion into his dying dreams, then suddenly pain jabbed through him as the face bent over him and its arms reached out to seize him. He came awake with a gasp, an oath, and saw the face—Plainsman brown under its stubble of beard and coat of filth, smelling of horse sweat and man sweat and fire smoke, but the most beautiful thing he had ever seen—break into a broad smile. "Come," it said quietly. "Outside. Litter. For you." Even the low, harsh voice with its halting Hond speech was a delight.

They moved south at a steady trot, the tough little Plainsman horses churning through the snow on the stubbled ground almost unhampered. Their progress was silent, except for the panting of the horses and the soft whispering of the snow thrown to either side. Every few minutes the leader's drum in the center of the short thick crescent formation would sound three sharp notes—*bum, bum, bum*—and back from the flanks and front would come *tapa, tapa, tapa*—the lighter two-toned sound of the scouts' drums. There was no jingling from the heavily padded harness and gear and, above all, no sound from a human throat. There must have been a hundred or more Plainsmen in the party, but for all the sound they made, their horses might have been moving across the moonlit snow ridden by as many dark shapeless ghosts.

After several hours, they stopped, and during the few minutes of that stop several pairs of rough but not unskilled hands were thrust into Wandor's litter, feeling the splint and bandages, fingering the gashes on his face and coating them with a pungent salve, and finally thrusting the neck of a skin bag to lips and pouring a strong sweet-sour liquid, hot and foaming, down his throat until he raised his hands in protest. It filled his stomach and its fumes seemed to rise up into his whirling head, and this time he knew he was in no danger of death. He was drifting off again by the time the drums sounded for the party to move on . . . the litter began to sway and creak under and around him.

For three days the ghostly party moved across the plains, and in those days Wandor could not swear that he heard more than ten words. Plainsmen on the march appeared to believe not only in not wasting words, but in not spending any at all. The heatless winter sun marched up from the horizon, slid past the zenith, and plunged down again, leaving darkness to flow across the world and the stars to stand out bright and icy and silent as the Plainsmen.

Wandor found the silence oppressive; above all, he found that no one could or would give the slightest notion of Gwynna's fate. He could not lift himself high enough in the litter to look for her; the only Plainsman with Hond speech among the party seemed to be the one who had found him and then vanished among his fellows; the ones who fed and bandaged him were good-natured but deaf as stones to all the languages Wandor tried on them. Gods curse them! Were they so harsh a people that none of them could guess what Gwynna meant to him, that none of them understood it well enough to call that one Hond-speaker and let him answer Wandor's questions as best he might? Would they be content to let him wonder if Gwynna was lying stiff and lifeless in the abandoned tent, lying until a blizzard buried her or bears and wolves treated her as just another piece of carrion? How long would it be before he knew?

On the morning of the fourth day, Wandor awoke to find that they were making a longer stop than usual, for some of the Plainsmen had dismounted and were building fires. Hunting parties of the scouts were bringing back small animals to be skinned and spitted. Underfoot the earth was firm but snowless. The grass was no longer a dead stubble, but gray-green tufts, and the air—somehow it now lacked the raw savagery of the cold of the northern plains.

Meat for the Plainsmen; winter grass for their horses. These seemed to redouble their strength and their pace; the litter swayed more wildly than before as the Plainsmen forced their horses up to a trot and then to a canter, hooves thunder-drumming on the hard ground, the whole band moving dark and silent across the land like a single vast beast with two hundred heads and twice as many legs.

Toward noon a hill swelled on their left and flowed past within a few minutes as the Plainsmen kept on. As it faded from view Wandor heard the drums sound again as usual, then a sudden four-beat: bum, bum, bum, BUM! And up from the center of the crescent rose a long pole with something red twisting at one end. As the wind of their passage spread out, it became a wide crimson banner with a gray horse running in the middle, then up beside it rose another banner still, a plain gold flag with a white border. A single long "Ha-a-a-au!" broke across the pounding of hooves, then died.

The western sky had turned the same color as the banners when Wandor felt another change in the pace of the horses. Now they were moving up to a gallop. The litter danced madly, till he was forced to brace with his feet and clutch as best he could with his better arm to keep from being bounced out. The pace increased, but now it was smoothing out into something flowing and mile-devouring.

Suddenly the air split apart with wild cries and yells and the neighing of the horses. All along the horizon marched blue-gray trees, but between them and the advancing riders glowed a thousand campfires, lighting up the shapes of ten times as many tents. Wandor heard answering yells floating up from the camp, and then the whole nearer fringe of the tents came alive with people boiling out to welcome the riders home. Men, women, children, babies carried in their mothers' arms, old men and women tottering along with sticks waved and cheered and raised joined hands to the sky as the horsemen came pounding up to the very edge of the crowd, drew rein, and began to spring down from their horses and call out to friends and family.

Four men lifted Wandor out of the litter. The crowd parted to let them through, the cheering subsiding around them. They carried him through a sea of silent, intent faces, into a brightly lit tent with a floor of thickly piled elk hides, and laid him down on a thick pallet of the same material. A sweetish scent arose from it as his weight came down. Then they were stripping off his clothes and the filth of a month's traveling through snow and water and forest and mud was being washed off. His bandages were at last being changed and a new, different-smelling salve smeared on his wounds. Finally, a pale-green steaming liquid in a silver cup was being raised to his lips. He drank it; the man who held it to his lips motioned toward the pallet. A sleeping draught? But where was Gwynna? "Gwynna!" he shouted. The man jumped, turned to a companion, muttered something in which Wandor caught no sense, then muttered something further, out of which sprang clear one recognizable word. *Zakonta*. Zakonta, the Red Seer. Would she know? Would she tell him? Even if the news was the worst? Would she? His eyelids snapped down over his eyes and his head sagged down on to the pillow as his mind slipped drunkenly into utter blackness.

XXIV

FOR THE SECOND time, Wandor awoke to find an unmistakably Plainsman face staring down at him. This one, however, was neither stubbled nor grimy nor smelly nor even male. It was that of a young woman, a large-featured oval with a wide mobile mouth and a strong wide projecting nose and enormous gray eyes topped by shimmering black hair. As he stirred, the eyes flickered his way and the mouth opened in a smile.

"Welcome, Wandor, guest and perhaps friend of the Gray Mares and the Yhangi. I am Zakonta, the Red Seer."

Wandor gaped as his own eyes traveled from Zakonta's face over the rest of her. He had expected some withered hag, like Kayopla of the Sthi, but this woman was hardly older than himself and only a few years older than Gwynna. His mind leaped at that thought, but the angry bull's roar he had hoped for came out of his throat a croak. *"Where is Gwynna?"*

"Here," said a clear voice from the opposite side of the tent. Wandor remembered Zakonta turning her back discreetly, then everything dissolved in an ecstatic tumult of pain and Gwynna's lips against his and her arms around him and his own blankets tripping him and his frantic babbling and hers and the saltiness of mixing tears. Finally his mind cleared, and to his mild surprise he was sitting chastely beside Gwynna, holding one of her hands with his better one, both of them looking toward Zakonta.

Before she could speak, Wandor said accusingly: "As guest and perhaps friend, might I claim the right to ask why I was not told Gwynna was alive during all the four days of our journey here?"

139

"You might, Wandor, and I will claim as Red Seer the right to answer you. After our rescue party reached you, Gwynna fell into the Seer Trance, which no man—and no woman not initiated—can distinguish from death. Had you seen her, you would have called her dead and we feared for your life if you came to believe this. The warriors of the party could not have explained it to you; they lacked the Hond speech for it. Nor would they have told you if they could."

Wandor flushed angrily, but this time before he could speak Zakonta raised a hand and shook her head. "No, we are not that cruel—not in that way and never to our friends. They knew of the love between you and Gwynna Firehair, because I told them when I sent them for you. But in winter, the Sky Demons hover over the northern plains and no warrior of the Yhangi will go there of his free will, nor, once there, will he speak any word that might bring them down upon him. When spring comes, and the Voices of the Earth Mother speak in the grass and the blowing wind, we ride north with laughter and singing and warcries. But in the winter, we leave the northern plains to whoever desires them.

"We would not even have been able to reach you in time, but that I tricked Jos-Pran into sending a party of a hundred warriors as far north as they dared go—to keep watch for you and be ready to aid you, I told *them*. To keep watch on the White Bulls, so I told Jos-Pran. He will discover my trick today, when he returns from receiving the tribute from the Yengkazili, and he will not be pleased. I do not fear his displeasure, but the two of you may face some hardship if he chooses to be as stubborn and disagreeable as is in him. He is skilled, proud of his skill, and also much aware of his responsibilities before the tribe; somewhat less aware of the need to temper firmness with discretion."

Wandor laughed, while Gwynna's laugh sounded beside him for the first time in weeks. "After what we have endured to come this far," he said, "a stubborn Plainsman War Chief is nothing much to fear."

Zakonta smiled. "So may it prove. You shall see him this evening."

The girl that Zakonta had left to act as their servant had gathered up the bowls from their evening meal, and was about to slip through the tent flap when it was violently jerked open from outside and a man shoved his way through so suddenly that the girl dropped the dishes in springing aside. With shaking hands, she gathered them up, took one look at the visitor, and slipped out.

The visitor was worth looking at. Not as tall as Wandor, he was as broad across the chest and shoulders, with massively thick arms. His skin was lighter than common among the Plainsmen and, instead of being clean-shaven as was their custom, he wore a bushy mustache curving down both sides of his upper lip. His massive head swung slowly to gaze at Gwynna and Wandor, who gave the signs and uttered the phrases of honor and tried to rise. He motioned them back to their pallets, then closed the tent flap tightly behind him before he sat down and began to speak: "Greetings and honor, Master Wandor. And welcome back, Gwynna Firehair—maiden no more—so I hear?"

"You hear correctly," said Gwynna, reddening slightly.

"I seldom hear otherwise. And it was by this Wandor, it was?"

"Yes," said Wandor shortly. He was not going to enter into a competition in bad manners with this man, but neither was he going to be any more polite than absolutely necessary if Jos-Pran insisted on beginning his conversations in this fashion.

"So. I am Jos-Pran, War Chief of the Gray Mares. Forty thousand warriors follow me into battle and they and all their kindred are in my keeping where their safety is concerned. I think it is in question here."

"Zakonta——" began Gwynna.

"Zakonta," interrupted Jos-Pran, "is our Red Seer. She has care over no more than our relations with the spirit world. She is but a young woman. With more wit than is common in such, to be sure, but still. . . . Though she was of the *Umnera*, the women who ride in battle, she can yet understand little of what concerns the safety of the Gray Mares or the whole of our people. Why otherwise would she send warriors north into the realm of the Sky Demons to receive two outland wanderers who may fulfill some prophecy that may or may not do anything but send the Gray Mares riding away to their deaths?"

"Because it is a true prophecy, perhaps?" said Gwynna.

"Perhaps. That will be Tested as the Council sees fit, but the Council will not meet over this or any other matter at

141

Council House before the last moon of winter. For now, you are *my* concern, and mine alone.

"Gwynna Firehair will go, as soon as she is healed, to the house of our Speaker; she will be under the care of his eldest daughter, Konbas; the wife of Nag-Oper, who will be directed to give her respect and honor and also exercise unrelenting vigilance. I shall take Master Bertan Wandor into my own tent, with the honors of one of the War Chief's Companions, and there I will also watch over him.

"Neither will have anything to do or say with Zakonta the Red Seer. Nor may they ever be alone with each other, without my consent, which I shall not give. These conditions I set that they may work nothing against the safety of the Yhangi or the Gray Mares. These conditions they will obey, under the penalty of being treated as enemies of our people." He rose. "Farewell and honor, Master Wandor and Gwynna Firehair." The tent flap closed behind him.

Gwynna let her breath out in a long whistling gasp. "Do you understand what he has said?"

Wandor nodded. "We are honored guests as long as we do his bidding. If we do not. . . ." he drew his hand across his throat.

"Actually they use an ax," she said. "But we can't afford to offend him. Even if he does not risk a permanent breach with Zakonta by slaying us himself, he can still so blacken us before the Council that they may do it for him or, at best, send us away in disgrace. But being apart will not be as hard as you might think, for I have felt—something, here"—she patted her temples "—growing between us these past weeks. If it continues, who knows?"

"Are you sure it's not something growing down there?" asked Wandor, gently patting her stomach and grinning as she blushed. "True, perhaps. But there are other things, which nothing in the mind equals . . . it is going to be a long winter."

XXV

IT WAS INDEED a long and cold and somewhat lonely winter for Wandor and Gwynna. But even the longest winters draw to a close. And it did not prove as lonely as Wandor had feared, for Gwynna had been right: in their minds, somehow—somewhere—a bond had been established between them.

Wandor found it (for a while, at least) a strange sensation to be galloping along the fringe of the Blue Forest with a hunting party, half a day's ride west of the camp of the Gray Mares, and suddenly have Gwynna's voice (somehow its unmistakable lilt came through even without sound) there speaking in his mind.

("How is the hunting?")

("Nothing so far. I think the stags have all been caught by other tribes or retreated deeper into the Forest.")

("If they have, Jos-Pran will be going in there after them. He's that kind. I only hope you don't meet any more bears.")

("Gods forbid. If I never see another bear in my life, I will be quite happy. What are you doing?")

("Sewing myself a decent hunting tunic out of elkskins. You know, if we could open a regular route over the mountains, those skins might be sold in the Viceroyalty for a good price. It would be more money for my father, and even more for the Plainsmen, so they would be less dependent on the Walled Towns.")

("Possibly. You know, I wonder what Jos-Pran would think if he knew how futile his hopes of keeping us apart turned out to be?")

("It would be a fearful blow to his pride. Best he never finds out. Good-bye.")

("Good-bye.")

The hunting party rode on. Wandor smiled to himself. Of course, in forty years' time if Gwynna had turned into a nag, this mind bond might be rather a hard thing on him, but somehow he did not think the gods would allow his Gwynna to turn into a nag. And if the gods did not take care of the matter, he would do so himself.

It was when they were returning from the hunt that day that Jos-Pran drew in close to Wandor and said quietly, "Master Wandor. The Council will soon be meeting. You and Gwynna Firehair had best be ready to mount and ride tomorrow, with the Speaker and myself and my Companions. And Zakonta. Your Testing time is near."

The ride east to Council House took more than a week, for the Speaker of the Gray Mares was old and white-bearded and not able to maintain the pace of the younger men and Gwynna. Still, they covered ground at a rate that would have done credit to any unit of King Nond's light cavalry.

The journey also did much to reveal to Wandor just what manner of man he had to deal with in Jos-Pran. On the fourth day, they came to Majoldyr.

Or rather they came to where Majoldyr had stood, until its people made the mistake of opening their gates to Jos-Pran's slave-traders. The walls and gates were still there; the house-sized blocks were immovable by any human power except that of the shadowy Empire of the Ancient Days that had raised them. But the houses and shops and meeting halls and market arcades were tumbled masses of sooty stone and blackened timber over which the molds and mosses were already growing and, through the cracks in once-immaculate pavements, the weeds grew freely. As they cantered past the main gatehouse, Wandor saw a fox looking out the window of the guardhouse. A lynx slunk along the wall and two owls perched on the crenelations at the top. And sticking out from beneath a mass of tumbled stone the skull and ribs and one arm of a bleached skeleton removed the final doubts as to the fate of the inhabitants. They had paid heavily and finally and totally for their mistake.

Wandor looked across toward Jos-Pran. The war leader was sitting straight in his saddle, his face impassive as his

144

eyes swept over his own work. Wandor looked back to the ruins—and thanked all the gods that he had walked softly and spoken low during that winter when he and Gwynna were at this man's mercy.

The Plainsmen usually distrusted towns and solid walls, but when they had need of them, they built well. The Council House was as large as four of their greatest tents together, and its stone walls rose two stories before the great peaked roof began. Before its iron-bound doors stood sentries from the Council Guard, the biggest Plainsmen Wandor had ever seen, holding drawn swords and intricately carved oil-fired torches.

Jos-Pran led his party in—himself and the Speaker in the lead, Wandor and Gwynna next, then Zakonta, and finally four of his Companions. The long halls before them were dim and gloomy, smelling of pine and old leather and oil smoke; hide carpets softened their footfalls and red and green hangings on the wall swallowed their voices. Gwynna clutched Wandor's arm. "I know they won't kill us, not unless Jos-Pran denounces us outright as enemies, but I'd almost rather they did kill us than send us back in disgrace."

"Yes. Send us back to see your father's Barony overrun and wasted, and die trying in vain to save the Viceroyalty for the King."

A sharp "Hush!" came from Zakonta behind them, as they turned a corner. Behind another door, red light and a low murmur of voices seeped out through the cracks. Jos-Pran stepped up to the door, knocked three times, and stepped back. The murmur within died, bronze wheels squealed and ground in tracks and the door of the Council Chamber slid open.

The low-ceilinged chamber was lit by long rows of candles burning in red-crystal pots and giving off a sharp musky odor. At the great crescent Council table, the War Chiefs, Speakers, and Red Seers of the eleven other tribes were already seated. Thirty-three broad dark faces, thirty-three pairs of wide gray eyes, thirty-three heads of long thick hair, some jet black, some gray, one or two shimmering white. Each trio had the banner of their tribe erected behind them; each had their talismans of office—sword, scroll, wand—lying on the table in front of them. Wandor felt his mouth go dry and his bowels churn and his tongue

145

stiffen as the heads rose and the faces and eyes swung toward them.

Jos-Pran and the Speaker stepped forward together, and spoke as one: "We bring here Gwynna Firehair, known to you, and as was written, the man who gave her womanhood, one Master Bertan Wandor. To us they came seeking aid for their kin; to you we bring them, to judge whether that aid shall fitly be given, or they shall be sent forth as bearers of false tales and entrapments."

Jos-Pran continued alone. He recited the tale of Wandor and Gwynna's arrival, emphasizing Zakonta's duplicity in sending the search party north. He told of the precautions he had taken to keep the two of them apart during the winter, emphasizing his concern that they not come together to work mischief against the Gray Mares or the Yhangi as a whole. He told of Zakonta's initiation of Gwynna, casting it in the most unfavorable light possible, with all the rumors about unnatural bargains and the like that he could dredge up thrown in for good measure. (Both Zakonta and Gwynna turned pale with fury at this last.)

Finally, he concluded: "Zakonta says we must grant Master Wandor a Testing, but she will not say what kind. Does she not know, or is she afraid that a true Testing might reveal things she would rather keep hidden? Comrades, we all know that Duke Cragor seeks vengeance against us for striking down his slave-raiders. We know also that he leagues himself openly with demons and foul spirits. What better way of entrapping us into his reach could there be than sending two of his agents (Gwynna choked with outrage) to us, with such a tale as has been told by these two—with assurances that their guardian demons will bring them safely through whatever we may set them, and give them the appearance of honorable persons who may be followed without fear? I may be called a trifler with the safety of the Yhangi for this, but who is to say that I am a greater trifler than those who ask us to give these people free rein to carry us where they will?"

This peroration had its effect; Wandor and Gwynna watched in horror as murmurings flowed back and forth amid nodding heads and hostile looks aimed in their direction. One of the War Chiefs spoke out in open agreement with Jos-Pran: "Send them forth and let us waste no more time with them or with uncertain prophecies and Testings. Slay them—no, perhaps they are doing this out of madness rather than a desire to do us harm. But otherwise, for us, if we accept them, what difference will their reasons make if we are led into the hands of Cragor the black?" He seemed to be speaking for far too many of the Council, or at least for many of the War Chiefs and Speakers. But the Red Seers were silent.

Zakonta saw this. In a second she pushed forward and called out: "My sisters! Will you suffer this folly? Will you suffer this thick-necked wind-swollen warrior to perhaps smite the gods with an open hand, and bring down upon us whatever vengeance they may see fit to send? A man is brought to you for a Testing, but you sit dumb and permit judgment to be passed on him in the first moment before the Council? Then you and I will all suffer alike the curse of the gods; our powers will depart and our people will be left alone with none to speak for them in the house of the gods and only the thick arms and thicker heads of such as he"—she jerked her head at Jos-Pran, who was spluttering incoherently with fury—"to save us."

The uproar that followed this outburst lasted for the better part of ten minutes, with each of the three offices divided from the others and within itself. Three dozen voices all raised in a ferocious din that made Wandor's ears ache and the candles flicker in their pots.

Finally the leading Speaker—his banner was black, with a green eagle bordered in gold spread across it—rose from his place in the center of the crescent and, amid the subsiding noise, said quietly, "Jos-Pran, we hold you in honor for your skill and wisdom in war. We hold you yet more in honor for bringing this matter before the Council, that it may be judged according to the Laws of the Yhangi. But we do *not* hold you in honor for your open desire to have us set aside the Law that gives every man brought for a Testing his absolute right to such. This Wandor so comes, and only with some measure of the gods' favor will he prosper in this Testing. If the gods have not utterly turned their faces away from us, they will not permit one who comes to us an enemy so to prosper, and Wandor will meet his just fate. And Zakonta speaks truly: the gods may find such cause for wrath in our turning away Wandor and Gwynna Firehair that they will deliver us into the hands of one who may come with a heart full of treachery and ill-will toward us."

The room was filled with a silence so thick that Wandor

147

felt he could reach out and gather it up in handfuls like wool.

Then one of the War Chiefs spoke: "So be it. I consent, and my fellow chiefs likewise. But what of the nature of the Testing for Wandor? Zakonta, is that written down in your books of magic, too, along with the rest of the nonsense about fire-haired maidens and their lovers?"

Zakonta's mouth hardened, but her voice was calm: "Brothers and sisters. This Wandor is a man of war. It is therefore commanded that he be Tested as one. Let him fight the best of our warriors here assembled, who will strive to slay him, while Wandor must fight to win *without* slaying. Do you consent?"

Enough apparently did, for the remainder was subdued into silence. Wandor wanted to ask who they planned to have him fight, but did not dare.

This question was answered soon enough. Jos-Pran turned a full half circle, bowing to the whole Council. With a thin smile, he said: "For this occasion, may I claim that honor? My weaponscraft is not less than any here, and it was my tribe, the Gray Mares, to which this Wandor and Gwynna came—or were sent. I claim this, as part of my duty, to guard the safety of my tribe."

"So be it," rang out a dozen voices, and Wandor stared hard at Jos-Pran. That treacherous young bull! All winter, he had been smooth speech and the forms of honor, and now he turned to murder under the form of a Testing! Wandor had too much battle experience not to recognize how nearly impossible would be his task—to fight a man determined to slay him, who would run any risks to get at him but who must not be allowed to run those risks, who must be kept alive at all costs!

"When is the Testing?" he asked aloud.

A moment's silence, then, from Jos-Pran: "In two weeks. If you succeed—well and good, for you at least. If you fail and are left alive afterward, we will not have to seek among the Walled Towns for the victim at this year's Northriding sacrifice."

XXVI

WANDOR LOOKED down at his weapons for one last time: bow and three arrows for the first round, lance for the second, scimitar and dagger for the third. All were weapons heavy on attack, feeble on defense; it was no longer a mystery to him why defeating without slaying was such a mark of weaponscraft among the Plainsmen, although to be sure their own normal duels seldom involved the use of all three in succession. Once again, he attempted to estimate the odds against him; once again he arrived at a figure too sickening to contemplate and abandoned the effort.

He looked down from the saddle, this time to where Gwynna stood, her face once more as white as during their ordeal on the northern plains, though her figure had filled out again and she was as desirable as ever. Which was *not* a thought to take into a death duel with him, he reminded himself roughly. Instead he raised a hand in salute, grasping the reins with the other, then looked across the level field to where Jos-Pran sat square and stolid on his own war stallion. Jos-Pran's hand went up, then his head went down, and Wandor saw the clods fly as his horse began to paw at the thawing earth.

No reason to wait any longer . . . he dug in his own heels and the horse started forward, pace smoothing out as Wandor urged it up to a gallop. Now for the bow; now for an arrow from his quiver. If he could make himself a difficult target, Jos-Pran might miss. And as for his own return shots, making *them* miss would be no great feat!

Suddenly there was a whistling and a sharp pain searing across his cheek—and then an arrow slashing through the

149

leather shoulder of his tunic and sticking quiveringly in the saddle. Jos-Pran was *not* going to miss; that first arrow had been within a hair's breadth of ending the Testing on the spot. It was best to close in, then, rather than be skewered out here like a wild bird or sacrificial animal.

He urged his horse forward, raising his own arrow to sight on the target. He had to miss the horse, for if he, an outlander, slew a horse of the Yhangi, he had been warned, they would at once put an end to both him and the Testing. Draw—Jos-Pran going for another arrow—judge the wind—Jos-Pran slowing for a better shot—Wandor's hand suddenly unclenching and his arrow arching toward its target.

And then Jos-Pran suddenly starting in his saddle and with curses audible even at Wandor's distance holding up his bow—its bowstring was neatly sliced in two—then dashing it to the ground. There were the beginnings of a stir of interest among the crowd.

Now Jos-Pran was lifting his lance; Wandor had two arrows left. Should he use them up or deal with Jos-Pran as the Rule of his own Order bid him and meet him with the same weapon? The second, to be sure. There was honor to be saved here as everywhere else a Duelist might be called upon to fight.

The two opponents came together in the middle of the field, heads bent, bodies stiff, arms entwined around the lance shaft, legs gripping saddle, and feet planted in stirrups as though they had grown there. Wandor saw Jos-Pran's lancehead of gleaming steel growing, hurtling straight at his chest, his own dipping low and to one side . . . and then Jos-Pran's horse jerked upward as one foot struck a stone. The spearing lancehead followed the jerk to crash along the crest of Wandor's helmet and snatch it from his head while Wandor's own lance slashed along Jos-Pran's belt, notching the thick leather and making him reel in the saddle as their horses carried them past each other.

This time there were gasps and shrieks from the crowd. As Wandor cantered back to his own corner of the field to dismount for the sword duel of the final round, he saw men and women looking at one another, then at him, and back again. And at this he felt confidence begin to rise in him. The gods had brought him to this Testing, and now they were working to give him victory over the mocking, doubting, blustering Jos-Pran.

Defeat in one round and a draw in the second had shaken neither Jos-Pran's nerve nor his eye nor the sureness of his arm. He advanced to meet Wandor, eyes fixed on his opponent's blade, his own half-raised, ready to snap up fully for an overhand slash or drop or cross for a parry, his feet moving seemingly of their own accord, cat-smooth and cat-silent, his other hand swinging close to his thigh with the fingers laced around the hilt of the dagger.

Jos-Pran's first stroke was as fast and hard and deadly accurate as Wandor had feared; sparks flew as his own blade parried it with a clang that rolled across the field and a shock that half-numbed his hand. He thrust forward with his dagger—and drew it back hastily as the point of the scimitar raked across his hand.

The next ten minutes were a wild flurry of clanging exchanges, with Wandor on the defensive more than two thirds of the time and never able to get in a really solid blow, whereas Jos-Pran drew blood several times. Once Wandor's foot caught on a tuft of grass and the blow that Jos-Pran landed then drove his guard down, missing his throat by a hair. He recovered his footing with a desperate effort and sprang back momentarily out of Jos-Pran's reach.

He would never get through Jos-Pran's guard with a blow hard enough to disable but light enough not to kill, even if such a blow could be delivered with the blade-heavy Plainsman scimitar. And he could have no hope of getting in close enough for a straight thrust with the dagger, either. He would have to bring it into play by what he had conceived weeks ago when he tested its balance, though up until now he had not expected to live long enough to use this perilous trick.

Now! A quick step to the right—one, two more. Jos-Pran kept his eyes fixed on the scimitar; the scimitar rose and slashed up and over, Jos-Pran's own scimitar rising to meet it on the end of a long thick arm, stretched out to the full, a beautiful target. And then Wandor's dagger hand snapped up and the dagger left his hand and buried half its blade in that arm.

Jos-Pran's grip on his scimitar loosened for a second, and that was all Wandor needed to bring his own scimitar down across Jos-Pran's blade so hard that it went spinning out of the man's hand and bounced across the earth to land fully five feet away. Before Jos-Pran could take a step toward it, Wandor lunged forward and his blade snapped across the man's throat, ready for a single quick final stroke with the slightest flick of his wrist.

Wandor had seen defeat in the eyes of many opponents. Now, but never before with greater relief and joy, he saw it in Jos-Pran's. Praise the gods—his guess that the Plainsmen knew nothing of knife-throwing had proven fully correct! The Plainsman leader lowered his head as much as Wandor's blade would permit, dropped his own dagger, and raised both hands. Wandor bowed his own head and thrust his scimitar back to its scabbard, while around him sighs escaping from the whole audience whistled and hissed like the plains winds.

The old Speaker stepped forward. Gwynna and Zakonta and the Speaker of the Gray Mares behind him. "Jos-Pran, you must give the first consent. Do you grant that Wandor has passed the Testing granted him?"

"NO!"

The Speaker recoiled so violently that he nearly fell backward on to the people standing behind him. When he recovered, he said slowly: "By what right do you claim that he has failed?"

"He has failed because he won by luck, the luck that brought his arrow to my bowstring and my lance to his helmet rather than to his breast, the luck that guided his cursed dagger. By *luck,* I say, and luck can come from the Sky Demons as well as the Earth Mother. Do you deny that?

"Then let him be put to some further Testing, where success will be clear proof of the Earth Mother's favor and hers alone. Let him mount and ride the King Horse."

The entire crowd gasped; a few irreverent spirits laughed. Gwynna started forward, murder in her eyes, and would probably have leaped bare-handed on Jos-Pran if Zakonta had not tripped her up and Wandor grabbed her and held her down until her fury subsided. Only the old Speaker remained still and silent, until at last the gasping and murmuring died and he turned to Wandor and said, "Wandor, you have been set a Testing no man before has ever been set, so I cannot say what will be your luck if you consent to it. But, although I fear he does this out of pride and arrogance rather than true concern for our people, Jos-Pran still has the right to demand this of you by the Laws of the Testing."

He raised a peremptory hand to still the rising voices.

"But I will permit this Testing only on the condition that, if Wandor fails, he will be permitted to live. The North-riding Sacrifice will look elsewhere, and he and Gwynna Firehair merely sent back over the mountains."

Jos-Pran nodded. "On these conditions, I consent."

"Master Wandor?"

"I, too, consent, though your conditions are merely a deferred sentence of death to myself and Gwynna. But when is the Testing?"

The Speaker looked Wandor and his various wounds over with a searching eye. "When you have healed fully and your strength is restored, not before. Two weeks."

XXVII

Spring was advancing too far and too fast for Wandor and Gwynna, to whom every warm day meant one more day toward the time when Cragor would put his army on the roads south of Yost. But nothing they could say, or Zakonta either, could advance the time of Wandor's final testing. It was not until the full two weeks had passed that Wandor found himself standing in a field of growing grass gazing at the King Horse.

The King Horse was by no means the largest horse Wandor had seen—Plains horses, like their riders, seldom grew outrageously large—but certainly the strongest and best-proportioned. Deep chest, long powerful legs, flanks full and rippling with muscle, long arched neck carrying a proud head with great alert eyes and immense nostrils, mane and tail as long and finespun as the hair of a maiden, and all over a silver-gray sheen. This was a horse for a king as well as a king for the horses.

Behind him, from the little gathering—the Council, Gwynna, and half a score of others—who had come with him, there arose a faint buzz of conversation. Was his hesitation showing? The King Horse stood quietly a hundred paces away. Wandor tucked the bridle more firmly under his arm and strode forward.

The King Horse continued to stand quietly, his eyes fixed on the approaching man, until Wandor was no more than thirty paces away. Then, quietly, with scarcely a sound or a wasted motion, the animal delicately picked up his feet and trotted off until the distance between them was the same as before.

Wandor sighed and stepped forward again more slowly.

This time the King Horse let him come within twenty paces, and then moved off again to his appointed distance.

Curses! That Horse would bring down all his hopes yet. He had no illusions about Jos-Pran's feelings, nor could he hope that any of the Council would stand against Jos-Pran, not when the Law of the Yhangi was behind the man. Gwynna might be another matter. If Jos-Pran insisted on smashing all their hopes, she might well in the end force him to take her life to preserve his own. What in the name of all the gods was this Law for? To permit such as Jos-Pran to wrap his arrogance in? To shield it from the scorn of the world? But all this bitterness would not win him the King Horse. He stepped forward again—and again his attempt met the same fate.

When this had happened five times his face was pale, his mouth was dust-dry, and behind him there was a continuous whispering, mixed with a few scornful remarks. Then one clear voice—Zakonta's—saying, "Enough! This is tempting the gods!"

And Jos-Pran's brutal reply: "The gods—are you *sure* this Wandor serves the gods?"

Wandor swore quietly, and, keeping every muscle except those needed to move his feet totally still, moved forward again. His eyes stared into that of the King Horse, who returned his gaze as tranquilly as ever and stood without a twitch or tightening of a muscle . . . nothing except the slow rise and fall of the mighty chest and flanks. Wandor dropped his eyes and moved forward again, the bridle dangling loosely in his hand. The King Horse dropped his gaze, too, down to the bridle. Then his head came up and, as Wandor took the final steps, the King Horse once more lifted his feet and in a moment was standing fifty paces away, aloof and alone as ever.

Wandor dashed the bridle to the ground and sat down beside it, while behind him the voices rose in gabbling confusion with Gwynna's ringing out sharply. "Never, Jos-Pran! Reject us before he consents, you will not——" And Zakonta interrupting her with low and urgent tones. Yet why shouldn't he consent? Was there anything he could do that he hadn't done already? How to mount a horse that wouldn't even let you get within an arm's reach of him? How, Staz, Earth Mother, how?

He lay back on the ground, feeling the prickle of the young grass, smelling the scent as he crushed the blades. That was a magnificent horse, there; it would have been good to ride him across the plains, the wind rushing past, Gwynna riding beside him. The picture was as plain as a painting in his mind: himself, mounted on the King Horse, the horizon rolling along before them, stopping sometimes to let the horse graze on some particularly succulent patch of grass. . . .

Something blew softly behind his left ear. Very slowly, so slowly that his neck muscles screamed in protest, he lifted his head. Then, even more slowly, he turned it. Finally, he half-closed his eyes and let them wander ever so slightly upward. From an arm's length away, the eyes of the King Horse stared back at him.

Holding his breath to shallow puffs, he relaxed his body and carefully stripped his mind of all thoughts and images but one of himself and the King Horse, riding. The King Horse shivered slightly and took two steps forward then lowered his head until it was practically resting on Wandor's shoulder.

He half-turned as Gwynna's voice rose again. "He's gone! I can't reach him!" What was she babbling about? Let him alone now, let him alone to ride this beautiful creature, this—yes, this *friend*. He conjured up a picture of himself standing beside the King Horse, brushing the long finespun mane while it nibbled oats and salt from his hand. The King Horse whinnied faintly and nudged the back of his neck.

He rose, and with no more effort than with any well-trained riding horse slipped on bridle and bit, adjusted them so they would give only the necessary minimum of restraint, then paused with the reins in his hand. Should he call for a saddle? As the thought passed through his mind, the King Horse shivered visibly; as he put the thought from his mind, the shivering subsided. Time enough for a saddle later. He grasped the King Horse's mane. It stamped once, then quieted. Wandor vaulted up on its back. Again a stamping; he pulled gently to the left and prodded with heels and squeezed with knees, and then the King Horse began to move.

He moved up from a walk to a trot to a canter to a gallop as fast and as effortlessly as a stone rolling down a smooth hillside. Before Wandor had more than time to catch his breath, the little gathering was receding behind them, and they were fulfilling the mind-picture of a few moments before, racing out alone together on to the open plain. Faster and faster they moved, yet the King Horse

156

seemed to make no more of a pace that would have reduced most horses in minutes to a blown and gasping stagger than he had of the gentle walk that had kept him away from Wandor. Sensations rushed in on Wandor—the wind cleaning the sweat off his skin, the long muscles of the horse knotting and loosening and knotting again under him, the high white-specked blue sky under which they rode over the plain.

It had to end; they had to return and see if Jos-Pran would now perhaps finally consent that Wandor had passed the Testing. Wandor put into his mind the idea of them riding up to the little gathering left—gods above, they were no more than a cluster of specks on the very edge of the horizon now!—so far behind. And he felt the King Horse slacken its pace, swing around in a great wide circle, and then return to its gallop.

When Wandor finally rode back to his starting point and dismounted, the entire gathering except for Gwynna and Zakonta was lying flat on their faces and a steady babble of prayers rose into the breeze. Gwynna was not praying, but standing so white and stiff that Wandor dropped the reins and ran to her.

"Gwynna! What did you mean, 'He's gone?' "

She shuddered. "When you were on that—*horse*—and talking to it, I couldn't reach into your mind! You and it together shut me out!"

Zakonta's mouth opened, but it was a moment before any sound came out. Then she gasped, "You—Firehair and Wandor—you have the Spirit Voice between you?"

"The voice that talks between our minds, when we are far apart and needs no spoken words? Yes."

Now it was Zakonta's turn to go down on her face. Then a familiar voice sounded, now strangely and agreeably subdued. Jos-Pran was getting to his feet. "Then my efforts to keep you apart were in vain? As if I were not already amply repaid for my foolish pride!"

Wandor looked at the War Chief, whose face was set like a rock as always, but now rather paler, and smiled. "Not foolish, Jos-Pran. If I ever have the care of a whole people, may the gods give me the wisdom to match yours."

"Above everything else they have already given you?" That was the Speaker of the Gray Mares, forcing a thin smile.

"They will do as they see fit," said Wandor. "Now, as I

think this ends the Testing, let us sit down together and devise means of dealing with Cragor the black."

This proved to be simpler than Wandor had dared to hope. Jos-Pran's shame diminished neither his wits nor his commanding manner; he immediately called a War Council by the simple method of commandeering the nearest tent, driving the occupants out, and calling in the other thirty-five Councilors and Gwynna and Wandor. There they, together, repeated their case, described their plight, and made their appeal. It was Gwynna who concluded.

"And so we *both* hold Duke Cragor to be a mortal enemy. Ride to our aid and that enemy will be confounded for years, perhaps forever. Refuse us aid, and that enemy will destroy my father utterly. And then, holding the whole south March up to the mountains, he will be free to move against you in any strength whenever he sees fit."

The choice after this plain explantion was clear beyond question, and without one dissenting voice the Council voted to send the aid. But there remained questions of *who* and *how*.

It was over the first of these questions that the debate went on far into the night. There were those who contended that the Gray Mares should have the honor, since it was through them that the god-sent Wandor had been brought to the Yhangi and revealed for what he was. There were those who said that everybody *but* the Gray Mares should send warriors, since it was through Jos-Pran's pride and stubbornness that the Yhangi had nearly rejected the god-sent. There were those who said that all the tribes should be represented equally, since there were opportunities for great wealth from this enterprise. (Here Gwynna, Zakonta, the old Speaker, and all the Red Seers broke into indignant sputtering at such a mercenary attitude. Wandor remained silent, knowing from experience that more good is accomplished in the hope of gain than out of purity of heart.) There were the partisans of one tribe and the partisans of another. There was very nearly a complete deadlock.

Finally it was decided that the Gray Mares had a strong claim and should compose the major part of the Plainsmen army. Other tribes camping to the west of Council House would also be invited to contribute, since they could be warned by Jos-Pran himself while returning to the camp of the Gray Mares. Those to the east would require special messengers. The Gray Mares would be sending as many as forty thousand warriors; how many the others would see fit to send no one knew for certain, for their War Chiefs said nothing. But there would be a host sufficient to sweep Duke Cragor out of the south Marches and straight into the sea— if it could only be passed over the mountains safely.

That the Plainsmen could not follow Wandor and Gwynna's route was plain to all. For a month at least the Zephas would be nearly impassable to any large force, because of the spring floods. Then the broad belts of forest and barren mountain might cost half the army's strength from starvation and tribal ambush. And waiting until the Zephas went down. . . .

"Nonsense!" said Gwynna. "Spring has already come in the Marches, and the Black Duke will have his army on the road as soon as they can march without sinking up to their necks in mud. They may not move fast, but they will move and if you wait until you can cross the Zephas dry-shod you may find the Marches an enslaved and wasted land strewn with corpses. Such victories as you may gain will be a waste of your warriors' lives."

"But we can hardly go through South Pass!" exclaimed one of the War Chiefs. "The Wall there is Ancient Days work—twenty horses high—and protected on either side by cliffs five times higher still. We cannot take it by storm, and to starve it out. . . ." He shrugged. "If time is important, there seems no way."

Jos-Pran spat. "Faint-heart! There is *always* a way! What of the Wall's defenses from the rear? It was built against attacks form the east, remember—not against attacks from the Marches. Am I not right, Gwynna Firehair?"

She nodded. "There's only an ordinary curtain wall with towers on the western end of the Pass. Once inside, you could easily seize the bridge."

"Then Baron Delvor shall raise a force to storm the western wall and move fast enough against it," said Jos-Pran briskly. "But for this, someone will have to ride ahead and warn him in time. Master Wandor, yours is obviously the best horse and you know the Baron. Will you undertake this task?"

"Of course," said Wandor. "And I can do it even faster by riding through South Pass myself and scouting out the territory. I can send word to Gwynna of what I find. With my beard and scars, and in this garb, I can readily pass as a messenger from one of the Walled Towns to Cragor. I can hardly imagine that the Wall garrison will be looking for a man that both sides have probably given up for dead."

"No," said Gwynna, "and think what my father will say when he sees you riding up to the Castle!"

"If I reach it," Wandor added soberly. "I think I had best ride as soon as possible, so that even if it is necessary to abandon the March, we can retreat to South Pass and hold it long enough to let you through."

"Good," said Jos-Pran. "You be ready to ride in two days, and we will be ready to follow you in four."

XXVIII

DUKE CRAGOR drew rein at the top of the hill and looked down at the army spread out below him. He had been able to override most of Sir Festan Jalgath's protestations about garrisons, and all of his allies' about the Khindi, so now nearly forty thousand men were marching south along the High Road. Soon they would be entering the south Marches and its vast forests; soon they would have to spread out and advance on a broader front to be safe from ambush. But for now, they were a magnificent sight.

Far ahead, already almost lost in the dust of their own passage, was the light cavalry of the royal troops—a thousand small quick men on small quick horses with swords and cuirasses and open-faced helms. Their mission was to scout and screen and probe and confuse the enemy. Behind them came the light infantry in their boiled-leather tunics and iron caps, shields and bows slung on their backs and short swords swinging at their waists. They would spread out the farthest when the army entered the forests, feeling out any Khindi traps and springing them and slaying the trappers. Royal troops and Cragor's own together, there were some four thousand of them.

Behind them were the heart of his army, two thousand royal heavy horse and ten thousand heavy infantry. The infantry, under Sir Festan's determined command, would march forward, their wall of fourteen-foot pikes bristling and their armor turning aside arrows to crash through the enemy's line. Through the gaps thus made, the heavy cavalry would pour, riding down the fleeing fugitives with lance and sword and battleax.

Except for a rear guard of another thousand light horse,

the rest of the army was composed of the motley array of infantry and cavalry levied from Cragor's own lands—here and in the homeland—and from those of his allies. The horsemen would be gallant on the charge, but not overly wise in the defense; the infantry would serve for little else but to occupy ground. Of course, when it came time to storm Castle Delvor, they could be pushed forward with the first storming parties and the royal infantry could climb to victory—and to the victor's privileges of loot and rape and massacre—over their bodies.

The royal troops! They were the backbone of his army and his plans to rule in the Viceroyalty; the gods be praised for having kept Sir Feston from seeing through Cragor's stories about the treasonable and menacing behavior of Baron Delvor! Otherwise, Cragor knew, he might have even now been standing on the walls of Yost, watching the royal troops advance side by side with Baron Delvor's men against *him*. And if they ever abandoned him now. . . .

"A good sight," said Sir Festan's quiet voice beside him.

"For every loyal man, yes," said Cragor. "But for Baron Delvor? I much doubt it."

Sir Festan shook his head. "I do not like this need to march against a man once one of King Nond's most loyal servants. Yet of all the lands of His Majesty, the Viceroyalty is the one we can least allow to fall into the hands of traitors. We can never allow them such a base!" He cast a sharp look at Cragor, whose expressionless gaze concealed an inward churning.

"Ah, well," said Sir Festan, passing on to other matters, "this is no concern for a soldier. I leave it to my masters to judge of treason. But I do claim to judge matters of war. And by your leave, my lord, I would judge it wise to send a thousand or so of your best cavalry, and perhaps an equal number of light foot riding on horseback, to move on ahead of us at full speed and seize the Delkum Valley."

"How so, Sir Festan?"

The old soldier pulled out a deerskin map and unrolled it. "Consider, my lord. The valley is some forty miles north of Castle Delvor, the last place north of South Pass itself where a small force can dig in and seriously delay or hamper a large one. Were the Baron—a good soldier—to think of holding it with, say, a thousand of his levies, and as many Khindi, it might cost us some days and many lives to root them out."

"Don't overestimate the Khindi, Sir Festan. Remember

how they vanished like smoke last autumn? They will do the same this year, if indeed Delvor has been able to bring any of them out of the woods at all, and if they do not—why, then, with the numbers we have, it will mean simply crushing them at a blow in the open field rather than rooting them out of their forest holes."

Sir Festan shrugged. "I was thinking less of the Khindi, who are, as you say, a small matter to an army such as ours. But what of the Plainsmen? What of the ride of the King's agent Master Wandor and the Lady Gwynna across the mountains?"

"What of it indeed, Sir Festan? If they did in fact make that ride, and neither perished during the winter or were slain by the Plainsmen, how can you suppose they would make the slightest impression on those unruly barbarians? If by some oversight on the part of the Five Gods they were to succeed in persuading a few thousand Plainsmen to march with and for them, how are they to get at us? South Pass? Nonsense. And as for the northern passes—*if* they exist—by the time they could bring an army over those into the Marches we will be sitting and feasting at Castle Delvor, with Baron Delvor's head stuck on a pike before his own gate!"

"All the same, my lord, if we held Delkum Valley, we could block them from coming very far north. And I still wish you had permitted me to send another thousand men to man the Wall at South Pass."

"Great gods above man, what's addling your wits!" bellowed the Duke. "Are you then so old you see Plainsmen under every bush and molehill?"

Sir Festan's face froze, but his tone was as level as ever. "Not in the least, my lord. Merely too old a soldier to risk exposing my men to obvious and easily avoided dangers."

"Oh!" Cragor burst out and spat into the dust. "For the love of all the gods . . . here, Master Kaldmor—come and tell this old fool that all of the Plainsmen are on the far side of the mountains and will be staying there for as long as needs concern us."

The sorcerer, standing enveloped in an almost tangible cloud of his own thoughts a little distance away, turned slowly toward them and replied in a low, even tone: "That, my lord, I cannot and will not do, for I would not be telling a certain truth. The Plainsmen are *now* on their own side of the mountains, yes. And I have heard nothing, any more than you have heard, to suggest that Wandor and their

Lady Gwynna survived their winter journey. But while it is not impossible that Wandor's protector and Gwynna's arts together failed and left them a prey to storms and wolves and Plainsmen, still I would not call this *certain*. And there have been such strange disturbances in the spirit world of late, such things as never before seen, that I much fear some surprise awaits us. I will do my best against it, but until the year is passed, I will not speak of *certainties* in this matter."

Cragor shrugged. "Have it your way, Master Kaldmor. But if you cannot speak of certainties, then speak not at all, at least not in the hearing of our army. And put on a more cheerful face—if you continue to wear that mask of doom, those who see you will conclude that you are frightened of something, and what frightens Kaldmor the Dark will be enough to send half the army screaming in flight back to Yost."

Kaldmor nodded. But his attempt at a cheerful expression was not overly successful.

XXIX

As FAR AS Wandor could remember, he had about another three miles to go before reaching the south boundaries of the castle lands. If it was farther than that, or if the south boundaries were no longer defended by the Baron's men, he had some doubts about reaching the castle alive. The King Horse was indeed faster than any other in the world, but he had been ridden fast and far; the horses of the eight men behind him—not too far behind him, now—were slower, but at the moment relatively fresh.

It was unfair and unjust to face being cut down this way so near the end of his journey. It was even more so when he considered how well everything had gone up to now.

He had ridden out of the Council camp before dawn one morning a week ago, with Gwynna and Jos-Pran and Zakonta riding beside him for an hour or so before dropping back and letting him go on at a pace only the King Horse could hold for long. They were to ride on at their own speed, reach the camp of the Gray Mares, and raise the tribe for war. That would not take long, a day at most, and then forty thousand and more Plainsmen would be on the march.

Wandor had avoided camps until he saw the peaks around South Pass looming up one morning, just after he had broken camp and begun the day's ride. He approached the high-walled Pass itself with some licking of lips, for here he was going to ride from a land where no enemy moved freely to a land where few but his enemies did.

The guards at the Wall were surprised to see a lone rider on a plains horse come galloping up the road to the bridge and request passage, but they showed no hostility.

And when they heard his story, that he was sent by an alliance of the Walled Towns of the Blue Forest to seek Cragor's aid in return for money and men, they smiled and nodded and passed him on without further objection. The garrison all seemed frighteningly loyal to Cragor; no possibility existed of persuading them to give up the Wall peacefully in the name of the King. But then, Wandor had hardly expected that the Duke, an intelligent man, would permit any but his most loyal troops to hold the most important garrison post in the Viceroyalty.

He had barely passed out sight of the Wall when the first group of riders challenged him. This close to the Wall, he could take no chances with a fight except as a last resort. He repeated his story. They believed him, praise the gods, and passed him on, although he had to turn down their offer of an escort against Baron Delvor's raiding parties.

The second party, and the third, believed him, for his route gave no clues as to his true destination. Most of the raggle-taggle horsemen Cragor had patrolling the roads were not overly inclinded to worry about a single rider or argue with such an exceedingly large and fierce-looking and well-armed one.

It was when he came to the fourth party, mounting guard over the small road that led north from near Jasnal Falls straight into the castle lands, that trouble finally overtook him. The leader, a squat greasy-looking mercenary, hailed him and said; "Greetings, stranger. What do you do so close to the lands of the traitor, Delvor?"

"My business brings me through here, on the King's High Road be it noted." Wandor repeated his story and the mercenary nodded.

"To be sure. I'd not want to interfere with a man on a true mission to His Grace the Duke, but still we've orders to escort all such as you beyond the South March, so's to give you no occasion for riding off where you shouldn't."

"Surely you yourselves can't be planning to escort me out of the March; it's better than two days' ride."

"Hardly, sir. There's other pickets every ten miles or so. We'll be sending ten along with you that far, then they'll send ten to the next, and so on."

If they had been planning to send only one or two, Wandor would have been willing to wait until he was mid-way, deal with his escort, and chance it breaking across country. But ten men were ten men anywhere, and there

166

was the road directly north, opening invitingly less than fifty paces away.

The picket leader had turned his side to Wandor while speaking, a careless mistake that was the last he ever made in his life. That life came to an abrupt end as Wandor's sword flashed out of its scabbard and sliced off his head as neatly as a severed bunch of grapes. His horse reared and screamed, opening a gap in the picket through which Wandor spurred, cutting down another man as he did so. . . .

That had been twenty minutes ago; his lead had been so great at first that he could neither hear nor see his pursuers. But that happiness had ended just a few minutes ago when he reached the top of a hill and looked back to see a column of dust with black shapes at its base come streaming out of the shadows into a brief splash of sunlight. Now he could even hear their hoof-thunder and warcries. If any had bows, they might soon be close enough to chance a shot.

There was a figure standing by the road ahead, standing so far out into Wandor's path that he had to swerve the horse around him, standing there staring up at Wandor as he thundered past. Out of the corner of his eye, he saw the figure—quiver slung on its back, bow in hand—great gods, a Khindi!—vanish silently into the forest. And seconds later over the horse sounds rose the mighty blast of a Khindi war horn.

Wandor swore as the horn was answered from far ahead and urged the King Horse on to an even greater speed. Had the Khindi risen against the Baron? Would there be a score of archers waiting to riddle him with arrows farther along the road?

He was so certain there would be that when suddenly the war horns sounded again on both sides of him and the air was filled with the whistling of arrows, he flinched violently in the saddle then composed himself for a warrior's death. But no arrows tore into him and behind him he heard horses and men screaming. He turned his head and stared.

Seven of his pursuers were either dead or unhorsed, and the remaining one was struggling to pluck an arrow out of his sword arm. As Wandor watched, another single arrow whistled and the man fell backward out of the saddle. Another air-filling whistle sounded, and then the road was filled only with motionless man shapes and horse shapes.

Wandor let out his breath and reined in the King Horse, then uttered a short prayer of thanks to Staz the Warrior. The Khindi might not be the Baron's friends, but at least they were the enemies of his enemies. He rode on more slowly.

The first thing he saw when he rode in under the gate of the castle and into the courtyard was a number of Khindi archers lined up along the staircase to the Great Hall. The second thing he saw was the door to the Hall bursting open. And the third thing he saw was Baron Delvor bustling out of the Hall and down the stairs, in riding cloak and hacked and rust-streaked cuirass, followed by Berek with Greenfoam in his belt.

The Baron came down the stairs at an undignified trot, which told Wandor a good deal more than even the pinched faces of the servants and the thinness of the horses and the camp of refugees just across the moat. If things were bad enough for the Baron to forget his dignity in coming to greet a guest. . . .

Wandor dismounted and went to meet the Baron, raising his hand in salute. The Baron returned the greeting and said wearily, "Welcome to a beleaguered and endangered house, traveler. Who might you be to come to us at this time?"

Wandor's hand went down into his belt pouch. Then it came out with Gwynna's ring, and dropped the ring gently into the Baron's hand.

The Baron reeled back as though struck, and Berek stepped forward, raising Greenfoam threateningly. And then he dropped it to the stones with a spark-striking crash and ran forward and dropped to his knees. With a wild cry, he embraced Wandor about the waist.

The Baron stared, his mouth and eyes straining open. "You — Wandor — back — where — how — help — Plainsmen—Gwynna." The last thought seemed to completely silence him for a moment, then he gasped in a great breath and burst out: "Where's Gwynna? Where did you spend the winter? Did you get help from the Plainsmen? When are they coming? How many? Where did you get those scars? Where——"

Wandor held up both hands to dam the flood of questions. "Gwynna is alive and well. We have secured help from the Plainsmen. The Gray Mares and their allies will be up to South Pass within two days, and can come through

168

to our aid, forty thousand or more strong the moment we take the Wall. And now for the love of all the gods give me a place to sit and food to eat! I've been in the saddle for the best part of the past week!"

The Baron was too amazed and confused to object to either the interruption or the orders. He nodded and began bawling orders to the servants, while Berek put his arm under his master's shoulders and helped him up the stairs to the Great Hall.

An hour later, with food and a bath and clean clothes procured, Wandor was finishing a hasty version of the winter's adventures—hasty, because this was no time for telling stories. But not as hasty as he would have liked, for the Baron had to be reassured repeatedly that Gwynna was alive and well. And when the old man had become convinced of that, there was another matter to be raised. "Master Wandor, has Gwynna, ah, *chosen* you?"

"She has, sir."

"Then let there be an end to this coupling in the woods like wild animals. You must marry her in proper form before the shrine of Kruga the Hearthmistress."

"I will, sir, if we survive," Wandor replied, biting back an oath at the Baron's apparently indefatigable concern for the proprieties. "And Sir Gar can officiate at a wedding spectacular enough to gratify him forever."

"Sir Gar is dead, Master Wandor. He received an assassin's dagger meant for me. It has made things harder than ever. And then there were all the men I lost during the winter. Too many—too many."

"I am sorry to hear that, sir. But can we turn to the military situation now, with your permission?"

The military situation was simple and depressing.

"Cragor's main army is only three days' fast march away, four or five only if we get rain and the roads go bad on him. His scouts have been sighted only a few miles north, near the Delkum Valley. I'm much afraid we're going to have to start bringing the refugees into the castle tonight; once Cragor's cavalry begins combing the countryside, the peasants will stay alive only on his sufferance. At least we can rely on help now, praise all the gods, including whatever ones the Plainsmen worship."

"Help, sir, *if* we clear the South Pass. How many men can you spare for that task?"

169

The abrupt change of subject left the Baron momentarily grasping for his wits.

"Precious few for attacking even the western walls, though that's all that we'll need to take it. Against a garrison of a thousand on that front, we'd need at least three thousand and that's more than we can spare without leaving the castle itself stripped bare."

"We'll have little enough chance with even that many," said Wandor. "We *must* find them somehow." He strode up and down the room for a minute, then his eyes fastened on the big map of the Marches spread out on the table. He knelt down on the rug for a moment and stared at it, then rose and turned back to the Baron.

"Here is what we could do, sir: we'll make our stand again Cragor's army in Delkum Valley—the north end, or wherever we find the most defensible territory—with two thousand men and all the Khindi archers we can find and get there within two days. We can't do more than delay Cragor until the Plainsmen come up. But if we do it that far north, the forces we send up for the delaying action will be able to retreat south into the castle lands and we can reduce the castle garrison itself to four old men and a boy with brooms. All the others we'll take south to storm the Wall and there we'll have our needed three thousand easily. Since we must have our men at the Wall before we have to bring them up to Delkum Valley, all the horsemen going north should give up their horses to the foot going south. That way the whole three thousand can ride and we'll save an extra half day and they'll be less tired when they get there."

The Baron was silent again for a moment, then nodded. "It's a risky thing, but if ever there was a time to take risks . . . so be it. I'll start giving out the orders at once. We can march tonight; you and I will go south and Sir Gilas Lanor will take the northern troops. He's a good soldier, that young fellow, and so are you. Gwynna's chosen well."

XXX

THE WALL LOOMED up like a portion of the mountains themselves, vast and dark and silent and grim. Almost lost in the early morning shadows was the Western Wall that meant victory or disaster for the cause of King Nond, a mere twenty feet high with twelve towers set along its mile of length. Also dark, also grim, it was less silent. From the walk along its top, and also from the towers, came the chink and clank of armor and weapons, the chattering of the guards, and occasionally an obscene taunt flung in the direction of the besiegers.

"Cocky, aren't they?" said the Baron. He looked around the storming party drawn up just outside bowshot of the wall. His instincts told him they were too few and too ill-equipped—barely a thousand, and not a single true scaling ladder among them—to make any impression on any fortification defended by such professional soldiers as the ones now looking over the walls at them. But he knew that instincts were a poor guide. Courage can often serve in place of numbers and, besides, what choice was there? He raised his hand, horns sounded, and the lines surged forward.

They ran as fast as they could, but before they had covered fifty yards the arrows from the wall were shooting in among them and men began to drop. The archers concentrated particularly on the bands of men, lumbering along with the heavy notched logs that served for scaling ladders. Log after log crashed down on to the stones as the men carrying them fell or tripped over the fallen. Some of the arrows had pitch-coated heads, and men screamed and writhed as the flames spread over their

171

clothes. From behind the wall came the *twang* and *whick* of war engines, and man-sized stones flew over the wall and crashed amid the advancing lines, dismembering men or smashing them into bloody paste on the ground.

Somehow, a few hardy souls made it under the shelter of the Wall with a very few ladders. These they tried to hoist into position, but as fast as they raised them, axes and poles flashed out from the top of the wall and tipped them down again, sometimes strewing the men climbing them with bone-smashing force on the rocky ground below. And of the hardy band that managed to reach the parapet, most soon came down again, alive or dead; a few dropped out of sight behind the crenelations, beaten down by a clustering swarm of enemies.

The Baron and Wandor made their retreat with the last of the survivors. The Baron roared oaths and threats at the enemy, his armor dented by stones and his surcoat pincushioned with arrows, blood trickling down his forehead from a flying rock fragment. When the last of their men had crawled or staggered or run out of bowshot, the two leaders turned to each other and shook their heads.

"We've got to find another way," said Wandor.

"What way?" replied the Baron. "If what you have told me is true, the Wall here will be cheap at the price of every man here including both of us!" He turned back to his captains and began issuing orders for the second assault.

The second assault was delivered and met the same fate as the first. So did a third. By the time its survivors had staggered back, some of them now shaking their fists in the direction of the rock where the Baron and Wandor stood, the sun was high in the sky—but over a thousand of the Baron's slim force would never see it again. Perhaps the men would have been less harsh if they could have heard their leaders arguing, and perhaps not.

Wandor was determined there would be no fourth assault. The Baron was equally determined there would be.

"All the gods forbid, sir!" exploded Wandor. "If we lose another five hundred men, and we'll be lucky to lose that few, we'll have barely enough to get us safely through Cragor's cavalry patrols back to the north and Delkum Valley! I tell you, give me a chance. There's another way—I know it! I only ask you for one hour, one hour to try my way."

"Some Plains witchery," muttered the Baron. "Very well. You'll have that hour. But at the end of the hour, every man still on his feet goes forward to the assault. Granted?"

"Granted."

Wandor walked over to a ledge where he could get the clearest possible view of the enemy's position. The western wall was everything. The barracks of the garrison stood in the open space between the west wall and the inner, true Wall; they would be overrun within minutes once a strong attacking force was inside. And all the gates and bridges and other devices were in much the same situation. Jos-Pran was perfectly right, up to a point. The Wall was indeed easier to capture from the west than the east. But easy enough for a force of two thousand, half of them already wounded, to succeed where three previous attempts had failed? Wandor doubted it.

He squatted down on the rock and emptied his mind of everything except the image of Gwynna riding her horse along the plains, with the dim shapes of the Plainsmen around her. He held that picture, then concentrated all his mental energy into it. The picture danced and wavered and vanished and Gwynna's thoughts came flooding clear and strong into his mind.

("What is it, my love? How is the attack on the Wall going?")

("As badly as can be, Gwynna. We're not going to be able to take it by storm, barring a miracle. Can you?")

("Can I work the miracle? Not alone. I——")

("Then call up whoever you need. Zakonta and the Red Seers and every priest and witch and sorcerer that comes to hand, and have them join to conjure us aid in taking this cursed Wall! Without such aid, we have perhaps an hour to live here, and then we die and our hopes die with us.")

("We will do our best.")

Gwynna's thoughts faded away, and Wandor, turning his back upon the men gathering for the assault, lay full-length on the rock and said softly, "Guardian of the mountain, hear me. Whatever help you have withheld from me this past year, while I met my enemies with my own strength, give it to us now. Otherwise, in the confounding of my plans there may be also the confounding of yours." He rose, brushed the dust and gravel from his clothes, and turned back to the men.

The hour was nearly up. The sun was now almost directly over the Pass and there would be few traces of

173

shadow left to conceal them, except what the few scattered boulders cast. Wandor could feel the tension, like a tightened bowstring, all along the line, could see the black looks that flicked from himself and the Baron to the wall and back again. His mouth was dry, and he drew out his waterbottle and swallowed a single mouthful.

As he was returning the bottle to its place on his belt, the rock under his feet seemed to slide sideways a pace and then drop two. His knees nearly gave under him. He stared around as the rumble and crash of dislodged boulders and the frightened cries of the men rose to a crescendo and then faded. A bird flew calling up past his head, then was silent. Even the men in the fort were momentarily subdued.

And then the silence was broken by a shrill cry, from the left end of the line, and echoed from the fort, "Oh, gods above and demons below, LOOK AT THE CLIFF!"

Wandor raised his eyes to where the hands were pointing—and his lips too formed a half prayer, half-curse.

Slowly, without fuss or haste or even very much noise, a two-hundred-foot slab of the overhang at the very top of the northern cliff was peeling away, tipping out into space as its weight overbalanced it, to hang for a moment completely free in a cloud of dust and small dislodged fragments, then drop like an executioner's ax squarely on to the wall. The earth shook again, more than before; wall and slab alike disintegrated into a mass of flying stones that sprayed in all directions like the fragments from an erupting volcano to patter and crash among the men. A hundred feet of wall had gone out of existence, with the men manning it—mashed into gravel and pulp. A great breach was open to the attackers.

Wandor's legs were carrying him toward the rubble before his mind was quite aware of it. When it was, he waved sword and shield and bellowed at the top of his lungs. Then he turned behind him for a moment and saw the men break out of their entranced and statuelike poses and begin to follow him. The arrow storm began, but it was scattered and pitifully ill-aimed compared to what had gone before. The men behind Wandor began to scent victory; war cries rose into the air.

The attackers came boiling up to the breach, climbed up, and poured over the top. Wandor found himself being helped up over tumbled blocks by two of the men, then staggered forward almost into a desperate sword thrust from one of the defenders, who went down a second later with Wandor's sword between his teeth. Another man sprang at Wandor, thrusting with a pike; one of Wandor's companions smashed him to the ground with a mace. The attackers sprang down into the open, waving their swords, screaming, yelling, snatching burning brands from the campfires to throw on the roofs of the barrack huts, chopping and slashing and stabbing wherever the slightest resistance showed itself.

It was all over within a few minutes—as Wandor had seen, once the western wall was breached, there was nothing more the defenders could do. That minority of them who did not die were too demoralized to try any destruction of the bridge or blocking of the gates; these were captured intact. The road from the Plains, the road of the Plainsmen, was open.

Wandor wasted no time once victory was secured. Baron Delvor had gone down with an arrow wound in the knee during the final assault. There was no danger to him, but equally no question of his being able to ride north. He grumbled and growled and muttered into his beard, but finally had to admit the facts.

Wandor consoled him in the hut in the shadow of the Wall, where he left the old warrior. "Consider, sir, how we need to leave somebody here who can speak to the Plainsmen—or at least, to Gwynna and through her to the Plainsmen. It would have been either you or I. And this way you will see Gwynna sooner."

"Stop consoling me like a fevered child!" snapped the Baron. "You know perfectly well that all the gods and demons working together couldn't have kept you out of that battle to the north, whether or not I was riding with you. Oh, well, I was the same at your age, if not worse. You've aged by more than one winter, out there on the Plains, young man—the gods have their eyes on you; that's clear enough."

The Baron was silent for a moment. "And of the gods—that earthquake was their work, yet I'll swear no priest or man among us prayed for such. I've heard of their answering prayers, never of their answering prayers not yet uttered."

"*Somebody* must have been praying for us," said Wandor quietly. It was all he cared to say now. And five

175

minutes later the King Horse was clattering over the rocks out of the western end of the Pass, on to the High Road, with fifteen hundred of the Baron's men riding behind, bound north into battle.

XXXI

THE CAMPFIRES circled the hilltop like a diamond tiara on a queen's head. It reminded Cragor of his wife dressed for a ball, the Crown Princess's tiara sparkling in her dark hair. Soon, now, with success in the battle that was approaching, she might be changing it for the Queen's. She would have the diamonds, and he would have the power.

Of course, there was the matter of removing King Nond before the King had a chance to do the same to him. If the old man had been unaware of the threat Cragor represented, he might have been left to die on the throne in the course of nature. But Nond II was far too shrewd and wary for that; he would have to die. The battle they would be fighting the next day would be a long step toward that moment.

Of course, Princess Anya might not be overly happy at being pushed on to the throne of Benzos over her father's body. But a woman's complaints could be ignored like those of any other domestic animal, even when she was a queen. And there were possibilities of pleasure, the kind Cragor liked most, in sitting down beside Anya and telling her in loving detail what he had done to her father—and watching her react. The picture was so pleasant, it was some time before he was able to shut it out of his mind and return to his tent for sleep.

Other horses than the King Horse might have taken Wandor north to the Delkum Valley as fast, but they would have been good for little or nothing after reaching it. But the King Horse was still fairly fresh when Wandor rode into Sir Gilas Lanor's little camp on the northern

177

rim of the valley. A good thing, too, for the campfires of Cragor's army dotted the hilltops only a few miles away.

"They'll be up to us tomorrow morning before the mist is off," muttered Sir Gilas. "Those Plainsmen of yours will have to move fast if they want to reach here in time to do more than avenge our deaths."

"They will," said Wandor. "I judge [he knew, from Gwynna, but again—a thing best not revealed] they were no more than twelve hours from the Wall when we headed north and they can easily ride all night if need be and arrive with both men and horses fit enough for battle."

Sir Gilas looked skeptical. Wandor laughed. "I know; you've heard nothing but travelers' tales and superstition about the Plainsmen. Thank your gods that you're about to find out what they're really like!"

They made a quick tour of the position—the tangle of wagons and logs and furniture and other bulky objects across the very center of the narrow valley, the archers posted on either flank up along the slope, the additional archers and the cavalry posted along the valley sides for hundreds of yards south of the main position, ready to launch arrows and assaults on whoever might break through. They found no fear, but no light hearts or spirits, either. Four thousand men have small enough chance against forty thousand, whatever the skill of their ordering, the wisdom of their commanders, or the courage in their own hearts, and not a man of the little army but knew that fact far too well for his own peace of mind.

Their job for the moment done, the two commanders wrapped themselves in deerskins and lay down to snatch what sleep they could before morning.

The crowing of the cocks in the few farms that had not been ravaged of all living things fell on the sleeping ears of Cragor's army. They had marched fast and far on slender rations, and it took all the kicking and cursing and threatening and blows that the captains and sergeants could muster to get the men on their feet and on the road again. By the time the clatter and rumble of a moving army sounded over the hills, the sun was well up, burning off the mists and exposing the green flanks of the hills. Both Cragor and Sir Festan agreed that there was no hope any more of a surprise attack in the dawn mist. This meant a straightforward driving assault on the enemy's front. But against such a handful as the Baron might have arrayed, did this matter?

Once the army was on the road, it moved along at a good pace, for the cumbersome supply wagons had been left behind today, circled into a vast camp in a clearing now miles behind and guarded by a thousand-odd levied footsoldiers against the Khindi who might otherwise slip out of the forest and try to take their share of such a rich prize. Sir Festan would have liked to leave a larger—and better—force, but the Duke overruled him. Not one man less than possible should march up to the battle that would win the Viceroyalty.

Even if the mist had still hung over the fields and woods, Wandor and Sir Gilas would still have been in no doubt of the enemy's approach. Not with the noise they were making, filling the morning air with it, a stable and a barracks and a thousand traveling tinkers all rolled into one—growing louder and louder as more and more of the Duke's army snaked out of the forest on to the cleared lands at the north end of the valley.

They were cleared, compared to the forest around them, perhaps, but still broken up with fences and haystacks and farmhouses; from some of these now rose the smoke of fires as Cragor's undisciplined levies wantonly applied the torch. To Wandor's eye, it was not the best patch of land for advancing over to battle. He said as much to Sir Gilas.

The young knight nodded reluctantly. "True enough, you've a soldier's eye. But it won't break them up enough, not likely, and if they once push a good force through our lines, we damned well aren't going to stop them with five hundred horsemen, half of them on ploughhorses and riding mares. Particularly if the royal troops—ah, there they are!"

The broadest part of the snake's body was now appearing in the open: a forest of pikes and halberds, swaying gently above a shimmering mass of breastplates and helmets, with the royal banner floating before and above it. Sir Gilas swore at the sight.

"The finest footsoldiers in the world, marching under His Majesty's own banner against His Majesty's own loyal supporters! Gods, how I hate to fire on that standard!"

Wandor shook his head. "Look who's riding beside it.

I'd fire on that man riding under any banner on earth or none." Sir Gilas looked.

Tall and grim on his black stallion, silver-spangled harness jingling, Duke Cragor led his army forward. His armor shone jet black, his surcoat and cape embroidered in crimson with patches and patterns of gold. His visor was raised, half-concealing the green plume on his head, and his bearded face could be seen turning this way and that.

Suddenly it stopped turning, remained fixed, gazing to the right. One black-plated arm rose and pointed; trumpets blared out brazen and harsh to be answered by the roaring and wailing of the Khindi war horns. A portion of the great armed serpent shook itself and split off from the main body—a screen of light infantry, behind them three thousand levied footsoldiers, marching straight at the most visible part of their enemy's position.

Wandor's mind reached out!

("Gwynna, the battle has begun. How soon will you be here?")

("Soon enough, my love. We will be no good to you if we arrive with our horses too weary to charge.")

("You will be even less good if you arrive after we are all dead and the Delkum Valley is held against you by the royal infantry!")

("True. But now leave me in peace. I have matters to deal with here.")

The bond dissolved. Wandor turned his attention back to the battle.

XXXII

CRAGOR'S FIRST attack, contemptuously weak as it was, came up the slope with frightening energy. Rabble that they were, the levies were heartened by the thinness of the lines opposing them, and of course, the royal light infantry were as tough fighting men as one could find. They came up the slope as fast as they or the sergeants' sticks could drive their legs along, the light infantry in the van and behind them the pikes and swords and boar-spears and axes and spiked clubs of the levies bristling every which way like a roaming patch of nettles. They climbed down into a sunken path, and up out of it, and then they were in bowshot and the Khindi opened fire.

The first ranks went down instantly, a horrible tangle of screaming men and thrashing limbs and falling weapons, but the others kept going—or their sergeants kept them going—climbing steadily over fences and hedges, slipping on cow dung, cursing and shouting, and screaming as arrows found their mark. A second volley of arrows flew, then a third, a fourth—leaving a trail of bodies, writhing or still, extended halfway down the slope now. The advancing mass seemed a strange creeping animal, wounded and trailing its viscera behind it as it reeled along.

Finally they broke. A handful of the light infantry kept on and closed in; the Khindi were at a disadvantage here with their lack of cut-and-thrust weapons. Wandor rode down himself and slew three of the light infantry. But the rest turned and, crouching low (which saved only a very few of them from archers who could shoot a squirrel off a branch a hundred yards away), ran back down the hill. Perhaps a third of the men who began the charge regained the foot of the slope.

But even before the survivors of the first attack had cleared the front, Wandor saw a second, larger mass of infantry, with cavalry on either flank, roll forward amid trumpet blares. He groaned. No number of dead among his own men would stop the Black Duke! He would go on piling them in, to certain death perhaps, but sooner or later the arrows would run out and then the full weight of an attack would reach the thin line of defenders and end it and the battle at one blow. To grind down the enemy, Cragor would spend five men for one; he could afford it. Great gods above, where were the Plainsmen?

From his horse, drawn a little out in front of the royal infantry, Sir Festan Jalgath had a good view of the battle, and he saw clearly two things. First, Duke Cragor was bungling his battle, sending his men (or rather, his allies') in penny packets against a position strong enough and well-manned enough not to be despised. The Khindi in particular were formidable beyond belief. Sir Festan had never seen them shoot so well or stand so firmly.

Second, even Cragor's bungling would not be enough to throw away the victory, for with an advantage of nearly ten to one (so Sir Festan judged), he could wear down his enemy at leisure and at whatever cost he chose to pay. Then a quick thrust with the cavalry and it would all be over. At the present rate, it might not even be required for the royal infantry to roll forward in their awesome battle formation.

This was not an unwelcome possibility to Sir Festan. To leave his own men intact, while expending Duke Cragor's levies wholesale, would give him a stronger position in the Viceroyalty. He could more easily restrain Duke Cragor, if such restraint proved needed, perhaps even strike out in someway on his own.

He decided to leave his men where they were. The less they moved, the less attention Cragor would pay to them.

What attack was it they had just repulsed? The fourth or the fifth or the sixth? Wandor had lost count . . . they followed each other as regularly as raindrops in an endless tumult of screams and weapon-clanging and bow-snapping. Before his army's position, the bodies lay so thick that one could have walked halfway to the forest without touching

182

the ground; they were piled so high that some of the Khindi were using them as barricades to supplement the fences and bushes.

Trumpets with a new note sounded—six, eight, a dozen of them. Wandor's head jerked toward the sound.

The cavalry was coming up—light horse and heavy horse in one mighty mass! five thousand or more of them, royal banners and Knights' pennons and Barons' standards cracking above them, the sun rippling across a thousand multi-faceted steel shapes reflecting painfully into his eyes. They were moving forward at a trot, and from where he sat on his horse, high on the rim of the valley, they seemed to be sliding toward the right of the loyalist line.

They were coming up faster now, breaking into a canter. The arrows were whistling out, clanging on armor, piercing horses that floundered and screamed and tangled those behind them. The mass wavered and churned and fragments broke off from the flanks. And then the Khindi rose, looking at one another and the enemy, holding up empty quivers and useless bows, rising, turning, breaking back into a walk, a run, streaming toward the valley. The other infantry stared for a moment, a few hurled curses, then their weapons went down on the ground and they, too, began to run.

Wandor sprayed curses in all directions for a few moments, then cut himself off and looked at the field. The right flank was gaping open to the enemy; once through they would race up the valley and block it. Backed up by the royal infantry, this blocking would be a barrier that not even the Plainsmen could overcome. They would slaughter themselves without hope of success: embittered and defeated, they would turn for home. Black disaster was rolling forward down there on five thousand sets of hooves.

Wandor made his decision. He shouted to Sir Gilas: "Ride! Ride to the left flank, bring them down into the valley and in on the enemy's right. I'll ride down with the cavalry reserve. We've got to stop those horsemen!"

The trumpeters blew, and the cavalry along the valley rim came streaming out of the forest. Wandor felt rather than saw them tightening up into formation behind him, felt the King Horse begin to stamp, and snort beneath him as the excitement communicated itself, looked around and saw perhaps six hundred men gathered behind him—and dropped his hand. The whole mass shivered and began

183

to move, the pace picking up to a trot, a canter, a gallop—six hundred men riding down to meet eight times their number.

Duke Cragor was grinning beneath his sweaty beard. Praise all the gods! Those fools were throwing their entire army against his cavalry. Well and good—that would leave the whole valley open. Send to Sir Festan now, have the royal infantry move up to block the retreat and clean up the survivors. He turned to Kaldmor the Dark and grinned. "Well, Master Kaldmor, what of your dark forebodings now?"

"What of them, my lord? The battle is not yet over." He seemed to be straining both inner and outer senses. Then finally he shook his head and cupped his hand to his ear to listen. And then he dropped to his knees and put his ear to the ground. When he arose, his face was grave.

Sir Festan was arguing with Cragor's messenger.

"Why should I move now, when the battle is all but won? What is there left worthy of my men?"

"Nothing, Sir Knight, merely that the Duke wishes the victory be complete."

"*That* is a sufficient reason? Very well, my men will move forward in a few minutes." ("As many minutes as possible," he added to himself.)

A low deep murmur and muttering began to creep up from the south on the breeze.

Wandor was fighting for his life.

The initial impact of six hundred charging horsemen is enough to stagger even a far greater force, and when the infantry of the left flank, Berek towering in their midst with Thunderstone biting a path into the enemy, came running up to fasten themselves on the cavalry's right as well, like a hound to a stag, the enemy stopped. But not for long, and certainly not long enough.

Wandor's light armor gave him little protection. Speed and skill alone kept him alive. Shield up to block a slash from his left, sword parrying one from his right, a quick thrust with the point now at an unguarded shoulder. The King Horse reared and plunged beneath him, lashing out with hooves and snapping with teeth like a war horse trained for many years. His sweat bathed him, his breath and his own stink filled his nostrils. Blood from a cut forehead, fogging one eye, *crash* on his shield, *clang* on his blade, an opponent dropped a mace from a spurting hand and tried to grapple. Wandor thrust under the man's gorget as the man lurched forward, and the toppling body almost wrenched the sword out of Wandor's hand. He jerked it free in time to send another sword spinning out of another hand, sending the hand flying after the sword. His muscles screamed in agony and his chest burned as though arrows and swords had already found their marks in a dozen places, his vision dimming and hearing filled with the crashing and shouting and a swelling thunder and roar.

And then the thunder and the roar began to develop distinct strains of sound—hoofbeats, drumbeats, wild chanting—and the heads around him began to turn toward its source. Swords and swordarms dropped back from around him. He lowered his own guard, turned his head, and saw it.

XXXIII

SIXTY THOUSAND Plainsmen came down the valley in a brown-black mass half a mile wide and long beyond calculation, for its tail was lost in the whirlwind of dust their passage raised. They came down the valley with the force of flood waters surging from a broken dam, and all obstacles shrank away from them, or vanished under pounding hooves. They came down the valley with the sound of elemental forces—the frenzied drums, the howls and chants from sixty thousand throats, the impossible thunder of sixty thousand galloping horses.

Cragor saw the valley suddenly turn black with horsemen and hazed with dust. He turned to Kaldmor with a scream. "Master Kaldmor, do something!" And then the Duke ran for his horse.

Kaldmor snapped erect and raised his arms in their long purple sleeves high over his head. His voice rose in a wild cry, "Toshak and the Four be served. Come ye, feed ye, slay ye these and serve me!"

Thunder rolled across the hills, and the birds of the whole forest flew up with screams and chattering. Above Kaldmor's head the haze that hung over the battlefield grew thick, twisted, and writhed loathsomely, and turned from white to gray to black to a virulent blue. It rose up now, like a snake preparing to strike, in a long writhing column, rising above the trees, above the hills, swelling at the top into a head. A head with eyes that glared red fire, a mouth that spewed black vapor, teeth that dripped slime, a great black crest that swayed and nodded as the mighty neck below it swayed and nodded to Kaldmor's bidding. Hoarse screams rose up, drowning the noise of battle. Kladmor saw the rushing horsemen waver and slow, and his voice rose up again: "Feed ye and slay!"

And the head arched toward the Plainsmen.

Out from the front rank of the Plainsmen rode two figures—women, Zakonta and Gwynna—and through them and around them pulsed searing white light, as all the Red Seers and all the Earth Voices of the Mother poured their power through them against Kaldmor. Gwynna's hair flamed with the light of a burning forest. Men who watched clapped hands over their eyes and flung themselves down as the lights white and red rose up higher and higher, swelling into a great dome, swelling toward the great blue-fanged head.

Light and head met, light and head wavered back and forth, and below the meeting place of light and head winds of hurricane force swept men off their feet and plucked at their armor and snatched away the words of their frantic prayers. The head swelled and shrank and swelled again as it battered against the dome of light. And the dome grew bright and dark and bright again as the head struck at it.

Then Zakonta threw up her head and hands in one convulsive gesture, and there was a noise like a thousand thunderclaps and a stench as though all the graves of all the earth had opened to spew forth their contents. . . . And then the head was gone, and only a pillar of foul blue smoke, drifting away on the breeze, remained to tell where it had been.

Cragor saw it all, and saw almost the end of his hopes of victory. Ignoring Kaldmor, who was limping toward his horse, he sprang on to his own and galloped up to Sir Festan and the royal infantry, standing as stolid and immobile as a grove of trees.

"Sir Festan! Move your infantry forward! They can still stop the Plainsmen!"

"And get them butchered along with yours? Bah! Here they are and here they stay!" Sir Festan turned to his second-in-command. "Find a good hillock and hedgehog up. Don't strike back unless you're attacked yourself. The gods be with you."

Cragor's face turned as black as his armor and his voice rose to a howl. "You refuse to lead the King's troops against his enemies? Coward! Traitor! Dung-spawned bastard!" His sword leaped from its scabbard and chopped

187

through Sir Festan's cuirass into his chest. The knight stiffened slightly, and then said very quietly, "That blow will cost you much." He crumpled out of the saddle on to the ground.

Cragor dismounted hastily, and was stooping to see if Sir Festan was indeed dead, when footsteps behind him made him leap up and twist around. A tall man in foot harness, with a mercenary's black-and-white shield, was coming up, sword raised. Cragor had barely time to bring up his own sword in a parry of the first blow; a second and third and fourth crashed down through his guard and rang on his armor, a fifth sent the sword spinning out of his hand, a sixth——

The sixth blow that would have ended everything never came. Instead, one of Cragor's guards ran up behind the mercenary with a mace and brought it crashing down on his helmet. The man toppled to the ground and lay flat.

"Kill 'im, sor?"

"Forget it, my man. Let him lie; save yourself if you can!" The Duke sprang into the saddle and dug in his spurs, galloping north as fast as he could flog his horse along.

Duke Cragor owed his own life to Kaldmor's delay of the Plainsmen, which at least kept them from sweeping his army away in a single unbroken charge. But there were few others in the army who had similar cause to thank the sorcerer. Except for a handful of fugitives who managed to flee into the forest (and most of these were rounded up within a few days by the Khindi), Cragor's entire army left the field either by Wandor's mercy or not at all.

The cavalry around Wandor tried to flee, broke formation, and were swept away like leaves in a millrace. The levies, both cavalry and infantry, met the fate of a crock of butter thrust into a furnace, whether they tried to flee or stand. At the end of two hours, the only part of Cragor's army still alive, let alone recognizable as soldiers, was the royal infantry, drawn up according to Sir Festan Jalgath's last orders. Wandor now rode toward them, a white rag tied around his helmet and another streaming from the tip of his sword.

They let him approach; the second-in-command came forward to meet him. "Sir Knight," said Wandor, "I grant you and all these men quarter; remain as you are until

188

those"—he pointed to the Plainsmen circling hungrily around the hillock—"have pitched their camp. Then march north as fast as your legs will carry you. I will not be responsible for your safety if you are still within the south March two days from now. Do not try to salvage any of your baggage, either; that is the lawful spoil of our allies the Khindi, for their brave and loyal service." The officer nodded and turned away.

Two voices hailed Wandor. From the left, Gwynna was riding toward him, her face pale but triumphant, bloody sword bouncing against her bare thigh, for she wore only the narrow leather loin-guard that was Plainsman battle garb for men and women alike. She reached him, and although twenty thousand or more pairs of eyes were on them, it was still several minutes before he released her and turned to the other voice.

A tall man in mercenary gear was walking uncertainly up to him, stopping occasionally to rub a bleeding head. He stopped a few paces away, and said, "Master Wandor?"

"Yes, and how may I serve you, Captain?" Then something in the man's voice pricked Wandor's memory, he looked closer, and his mouth opened and closed several times before he exclaimed, "Count Arlor!"

"Indeed," said the man. "We had heard nothing of you for so long, over in Benzos, that His Majesty sent me over here to find out how you had been spending your time." He looked from Wandor to Gwynna to Berek to the Plainsmen and the Khindi drifting past and to the corpse-strewn field and the royal infantry standing like a stranded ship above them all. Then he grinned and turned back to Wandor. "I will report to His Majesty that you have been spending your time very usefully indeed."

"I sincerely hope so."

"You need not hope. If Cragor got more than one tenth of the men he can rely on clear of this shambles, it's a miracle. And how much he can rely on the royal infantry, after butchering their commander, I don't know."

"Do you think this will end Cragor's plotting?"

"Hardly. But it will mean at least another year before he can give further effect to any of his plots, at least here in the Viceroyalty."

"A year," murmured Wandor, looking at Gwynna. He knew he was launched on a road that had no turning back nor any apparent goal. A road full of dangers against which his own strength and skill might be hardly sufficient guard.

A road where yet more tokens from the Testing set him by the Guardian of the Mountain might appear. But it was a road that he would not have to walk alone; Gwynna would be with him.

THE EXPLOSIVE, RIOTOUS NOVEL OF
WAR AND PEACE...
LOVE AND HATE...
BATTLE SCENES AND SEXY WOMEN!

WORLD WAR III

BY
JOHN STANLEY

On the stretches of Mainland China, in the all-too-
probable future, two terrifying forces are at war: the
Chinese People's Liberation Army and the regular
U.S. Forces.

Neither side though, has reckoned with the might
of Squad C-323, killer chimpanzees—Kong, Son of
Kong, Bonzo, Sgt. Joe Young—whose battle action
would turn the tide and once again make the world
safe ... for something!

"Fantasy, allegory, satire—a multi-level
book by a multi-talented writer. John
Stanley has shown the nightmare behind
the dreams of glory and given us an un-
forgettable glimpse of the rape of things
to come." Robert Bloch, author of PSYCHO

 26872 $1.95

WWIII 1-76

AVON ◆ MEANS THE BEST IN FANTASY AND SCIENCE FICTION

URSULA K. LE GUIN

The Lathe of Heaven	25388	1.25
The Dispossessed	24885	1.75

ISAAC ASIMOV

Foundation	23168	1.25
Foundation and Empire	23176	1.25
Second Foundation	23184	1.25
The Foundation Trilogy (Large Format)	26930	4.95

J. T. McINTOSH

Flight from Rebirth	03970	.75
The Suiciders	17889	.75
Transmigration	03640	.75

ROGER ZELAZNY

Creatures of Light and Darkness	27821	1.25
Lord of Light	24687	1.50
The Guns of Avalon	24695	1.25
Nine Princes in Amber	27664	1.25
The Doors of His Face, The Lamps of His Mouth	18846	1.25

Include 25¢ for handling, allow 3 weeks for delivery.
Avon Books, Mail Order Dept.
250 W. 55th St., N.Y., N.Y. 10019

SF 11-75